I0749591

Lacy is in a panic state of mind. "I can't believe I screwed up my life so badly to the point of putting my family's life in danger. I have let beauty and sex almost, destroy my life." Lacy doesn't seem to know which way to turn or who he can talk to about the big mess he has gotten himself into. "My best friend's wife is my wife's best friend which will really complicate this situation for me if I confided in him. Of course, since he is a lawyer I can ask him to take me as a client and everything will be confidential at that point."

"I know there's that old saying, "a grown man is not suppose to cry" but I cry every night. It's a lonely life for me without my wife in bed next to me, and I lie there, crying in the dark. I let my strong desire for a little sample of something different from what I thought I didn't have at home cause me this much pain and suffering. I want my wife Imani and my twin daughters Lacey and Stacey back as a, family, and I will get them back. I will never stop trying."

When love hurts, it hurts.

When love hurts you know, it just ain't no good
Yet you keep hoping and doing all you possibly could
Knowing that your stuff is roaming for another's connection
Acting like a dog in heat with no damn affection or direction
Lust is a hell of a thing when you can't control your shit
And yet still, there's that strong desire to hump a little bit
But as we already know, it doesn't last forever
Good sense kicks in and he knows home nest is better
Now he's running home with his tail between his "ass"
Stead-fast praying for a chance to forever make it last
And if home is no longer there for him to claim
Maybe hurting love just ain't worth the pain.

HURTING LOVE
HURTING LOVE

Haywood Publishing, LLC
P.O. Box 1420
Detroit, MI 48235

Published by, Haywood Publishing, LLC

Original front cover picture design by:
Steven Reed

Second printing: September, 2012

Library of Congress Cataloging-in-Publication Data has been applied for:

ISBN 978-0-9768820-1-5 (previously ISBN 978-1475231991)

9 8 7 6 5 4 3 2 1
Printed in the United States of America

Dedications

……………………..

I dedicate this book with much love and appreciation to my children. They always keep me uplifted with encouragement to keep my dream/passion alive. To my sands, they are the true meaning of the word, soror. To my friend out there in Las Vegas, here's the book you've been waiting for, I hope you like it, and also, thanks for the big lunch at the restaurant and the unforgettable tour of the city you gave me and your aunt when we attended a conference there. To very dear people, who will always be in my heart as well as a part of me, my friends at Detroit's Unity Poets and Authors Society (DUPAAS), and last but not least, "Always and, Forever."

Acknowledgements

I give special thanks to Michigan Chronicle News for my exposure to a multitude of readers during the year, 2010. I was very much pleased and very happy to learn that readers of the paper were following my writing of poetry each week. Thc exposure gave me a wide spread audience.

I also give heartfelt thanks to my friend and the person I call my brother, Arvis Perry, for making it all possible.

Preface

....

The title, Hurting Love, is a strong statement within itself. It may be thought of in a negative way but, once the reader gets into this book it will be perfectly clear to the reader that it is a story that depicts the lives of married couples with well-rounded, family life settings. As always, there are ups and downs as well as good and bad in people's lives on general basic. It's the negative side that, when changed, can bring about the appreciation of the positive side in a person's life. You, my dear readers, will enjoy the families as a whole. The children are always a joy to behold, they add plus energy to a loving home. And, like most married couples within their private compounds, there's plenty love and love making going on and there will be little misunderstandings that will bring on little spats as in average households. It all comes together for the sake of good. And, still life goes on.

In this book I went outside the marriage and highlighted the forbidden fruit, and, as you get into this book you will see how people's lives can take a turn for the worse from just one mistake that got out of hand. I know that each and every one of you, my dear readers, will greatly enjoy this book.

"HAPPY READING"

HURTING LOVE

Floria "Diva 007" Willis

HAYWOOD PUBLISHING, LLC

haywoodpublishing@sbcglobal.net

Website

www.haywoodbooks.com

!!

WHEN LOVE HURTS, IT HURTS

!!

Best Friends, Lunch, Chit-Chat and Laughter

Welcome to the "D"

....

Rrrrrring, rrrrrring, rrrrrring…, "hello…, girl I was about to call you. Monique where are you?" "On my way to pick you up, I have a few errands this morning but I can finish after lunch." "No, I will drive myself, just tell me where and what time and I will see you there." Less than an hour Monique and Imani were together at their favorite Restaurant in Downtown Detroit ordering a big lunch. "Imani I got a taste for Alligator today, and you do know how I love my Gator. Whether it's fried or smothered in onion gravy served over rice, it's all deliciously good. I'll just add it to my order and we can share since it is more than one person can eat. Leftover gator meat is not quite as good anyway." The ladies engaged in good conversation over lunch. It is too early in the day to go to their favorite watering hole but that can be another kind of sister girl best friends' kind of date with great conversation that is not about business.

Monique Haywill and Imani Ball are best friends. They have known each other since kindergarten and have remained friends throughout their college days and on into the present. It is amazing how they met and married two best friends, Tyrone Haywill and Lacy Ball. The men, after passing the Bar Exam, had gone into partnership opening a law firm that became very profitable.

"Monique, what are your plans for the weekend?" "Imani, it's big, I got plans laid out for the whole weekend, just me and Tyrone. We are planning a mini honeymoon right there at the crib. What's going on with you and Lacy for the weekend?" "Nothing, Lacy has been working late and he has been tired most of the time when he gets home. I just try to make things comfortable for him. He doesn't have time for the twins anymore either." "Imani, look at the time, I hate to rush this way but I need to do something before my kids get out of school. The lunch was great, but I will have to take this bread pudding in a carryout. It is good to eat anytime. I will call you next week about a lunch date and maybe we'll have lunch at one of the

casinos. I don't gamble but I will eat there." "I'll be looking forward to next time Monique and if something should come up, I will call you." As the ladies exit the restaurant Monique purposely didn't mention husbands or the weekend anymore. "If there's something going on in Imani's home life
I'll wait and let her confide in me, and I know she will when she is ready." The ladies said their goodbyes on the parking lot and got into their cars and headed out in different directions.

LOVE, LIES, AND MORE LOVE AND LIES

....

Monique is all smiles as she ponders over what is happening with her and the love of her life, Tyrone. "Oh what a beautiful day this is going to be for me and my Heavenly-blessed soul mate. HEY, Everybody! I love my man." Here it is the weekend with today being Saturday and no job to go to and on top of all this I am enjoying my kind of weather. It's my special kind of day. It is a cloudy day and raining, plus the rain beating against my window pane has driven my sexual drive to the sky. Knowing me and saying that can be an understatement if I must say so myself. I know my man and we both know it is going to be an explosion in our bedroom this morning. After we have made love, Tyrone sweetly squeezes me and says, "my wife, my wife. Sometimes when we're together this way I forget to muffle his loud sounds and I always feel so embarrassed when the kids see us later and look at us in a puzzled strange kind of way. Monique lay staring at the ceiling with beautiful thoughts going on in her head as she continued in thought.

"This is a great, on target husband and wife weekend, and I'm enjoying every minute of it.
The look I see on Mr. Haywill's face shows pure joy." Monique finally got up and started moving around, trying not to disturb Tyrone so early. "Hey baby, why are you up so early? Today is Saturday in case you've forgotten, and there's no work for me today." "Tyrone, I'm going to check on the kids and prepare breakfast for us. I will join you later and you can have breakfast in bed." "Monique, you can make that breakfast for two." "You got it, boss. See you later." "Monique, don't forget to check with your assistant at the boutique. It was a wise decision to hire someone to keep things going when you're not there."

Monique mumbles, "that man and I are meant for each, other. When God put two people together, you know it's real. It smells real, it taste real, and the essence of it is spiritually real."

EARLY SUNDAY MORNING

....

It is Sunday morning and Monique is tired but she must hurry so she will not be late for church service. "I do not like missing the beginning of the sermon. "Pastor Jones knows that his Sunday messages carry me through the rest of the week. If I cannot recall all that he's delivered, I will play the CD I purchased on my way out the door after the service."

"As I look around my home and at my family I can truly say that I am a happy woman"; then, Monique adds, "I am blessed because the Lord has given me a beautiful family."

"My husband has always been proud of his children and it is obvious that they are his world.
He always seems to get a big kick out of being able to say, "our children look just like me"; He, then throws in that punch line where he says, "would you like to try for a, "you look alike?" Like always, I would give him that kind of look that says "unless you can give birth, HELL NO."

"Here I am, Mrs. Tyrone Haywill, as I sometime call myself after our lustful, prolonged weekends together." Lord, get me to church on time, is Monique's thought as she try to put aside the thought of all the energy that she released yesterday and early this morning before stumbling to the kitchen for a cup of hot coffee to get her going for the day. "This has truly been a beautiful, terrific, right-on-target, soul-mate weekend for Tyrone and me." Monique continued to be in deep thought.

"You can believe me when I say it has not always been this way with me and Tyrone. Here in Detroit, Michigan our summers can be as hot as our winters are cold, and Detroit doesn't go half-ass with nothing, not even the weather, and if you don't like the weather, wait a minute."

"It was a hot summer day, the month of July, and one of our city's extremely hot days when Tyrone and I decided to go for a ride in his car. "Monique, it has been a while since we've cruised around, stopping at different sights, enjoying ourselves with just the two of us." "I know, Tyrone and it feels good having this time to ourselves. Let's add this to our Family Tradition." "Monique, starting today it is a Family Tradition added on." While riding along we had barely left the street in our up-scale neighborhood when I just happened to do something out of the norm by looking in his glove compartment. Laying there on top of everything else I saw a picture of a woman in a compromising position that is meant for the eyes of the man only. Before I could ask who the person is, Tyrone snatched the picture out of my hand and threw it out the window. He started cursing, "That damn Lacy borrows my car and leaves his whore's picture in my glove compartment. Oh, his ass is mine." The attention I got that night made me forget all about the picture. If there's a payday in Tyrone's future, he knows his will be a "mother" and if someone is stirring in my pot, Tyrone knows that I'm like a hound dog. I must try to remember that, with Tyrone being a lawyer, he might be in compromised positions all the time because some women misread his smooth actions and sexy voice along with a smile that would stop a woman in her tracks. Both attorneys are so much alike in their smooth talking ways that is why I keep up with home front. I don't want other women pushing up on my man, that is why I don't push him out there to get his ego stroked by desperate single women nor the unsatisfied married ones. If my husband needs a little sexual attention in the middle of the day he knows that all he has to do is call me." Monique's thoughts are working back to back this morning; when suddenly reality sets in. "My husband was lying through his teeth. Tyrone Haywill must and will pay for having that picture in his, my, our car." Monique's thought is, someday, someday, someday, just you wait, someday, someday, someday.

"Here I am rushing into the church, hoping that I am looking my best because I like to look beautiful in HIS house while listening to HIS words. I know whatever I wear is just fine at my church, but I personally like to look f-i-n-e. After church I will go home and spend the rest of the afternoon and evening with my husband and children. Ty, Jr. and Angel left early for Sunday School with the parents of their friends. Tyrone always has dinner ready for me and the kids when we get home from church. It would be nice if he would go to church with us sometimes. I have not been able to get him to go with us, but I am still trying and I will continue to try. I sometimes try to lay that guilt trip on my husband by saying to him that if he does not fellowship with other Christians at least once or twice a week it means that he is playing favorites with the devil, and visiting for programs do not count. That man had the nerve to say to me," "I am with you all the time so that should count." "I told him all he is doing is buying a first class ticket to the final resting place for Satan's followers." Monique's thoughts had become verbal and she quickly checked herself. Finally, Monique is seated and she's not very late, they just starting taking up collection. After a beautiful service, Monique headed out for the long drive home on a beautiful sunny day.

FLASHBACKS FROM THE PAST
A NIGHT OUT WITH THE BOYS

....

It's 3:00 a.m. in the wee hours of the morning and flashbacks suddenly enters Monique's mind. It's about the time Tyrone would be late coming home and the first words that came from his mouth was, "Baby, I was out with the boys." She would read him his rights like a strong black woman and ask him, "Which one of the boys had a split between his legs?" That same flashback keeps coming back with no comfort to what Monique is feeling. Tyrone had no idea what he was putting her through back then.

The man is so good at what he does, he captivated Monique's heart the very first time they met. Mr. Tyrone Haywill was standing strong like a stud in Monique's eyes. She called him her Black Stallion. She was so into him, she could have eaten a half pound of his chicken hockey without even a fraction of a thought. Whatever the man is doing, it must be good because he would have her talking to herself, and sometimes answering herself. Could his joystick be that damn good?

Monique has no idea why she keeps having the same flashbacks over and over again. No matter how many times it comes back to her, it doesn't hurt any less. All it ever brings to her is more hurt and more tears. The crazy part of it all is, Tyrone needs only to pull her close to him and caress her and thrush his loins inside her, and again she is at his mercy for hurt all over again. She also knows that Tyrone loves her very much and wouldn't hurt her on purpose. Whatever the reason for his actions she knows that it will come to pass because nothing that has been touched by the Holy Spirit can remain in the dark. Their marriage was built on the Word, but somewhere along the way things changed and it still leaves her sometimes suspicious and feeling hurt. It might help if she understood the actions.

THINKING ABOUT THE PAST THE WAY IT USE TO BE

……………………………………

"Tyrone, why are you, sneaking in the bedroom 3:00 A.M. in the morning? I am wide awake and I can see your guilty ass." "Monique baby, I was hanging out with the boys and I stayed longer than I had planned." "I was sweet as I handled my business;" Monique spoke softly, "Come to bed. I was having a romantic dream about us and reached over but, "no you." "Sweetheart I have been waiting for you and I need you now; all the time I was thinking, I want to see him and it, so I turned on the brightest light in the bedroom and waited for him to come with an excuse for why he can't or doesn't want to perform on and with me right now. Tyrone stepped up to the bed showing Master Jones and it was standing up there so proud, as if it had not seen or felt anyone since me. I could not believe this man, and now I can't call it off because Master Jones is ready, and I want to scream out everything but the shout of ecstasy."

Monique can look back and laugh at all the incidents except one. It's the one where she had to say out loud, "oh no the hell she didn't!" It all happened while she was at her Boutique on Father's Day weekend. Flowers were sent to their home and their babysitter Mrs. Bibi signed for the delivery. Tyrone had heard the doorbell and went to see who was calling. As Mrs. Bibi turned around….

"Oh, you startled me Mr. Haywill, these flowers were just delivered, and they're for you." Tyrone retrieved the card and flowers quickly from Mrs. Bibi and hurried back to the master bedroom. Monique never got to see the flowers, however her husband had an interesting story to tell, her. Somehow a mistake was made with the delivery and the flowers were delivered to the wrong address. she can understand that an error could be made during a busy weekend of declaring and showing love and spreading love. She's with showing love myself, so she's down with that. Tyrone, being a good honest person took it upon himself to take the flowers to the flower shop that had the name and address on the card. However, Monique found out later that Mrs. Bibi and Ty, Jr. observed Tyrone taking the flowers outside but not to his car, instead he went straight to the garbage container and threw them in it." Ty Jr. asked, "Mama, why did daddy throw the pretty flowers in the garbage can?" It would have helped if he had said something before garbage pickup which took place the very next day after Father's day."

"You know this had to be about the time Monique would say, "no-the-hell they didn't. I can understand the bitch being trifling but I will not accept it from my husband. Whoever he was doing, I guess he had to put her on the back burner after coming so close to hell, which I would have put him through with vengeance." For Monique, this will never come back laughable because someone crossed the line by disrespecting the Haywill mansion which is her home.

AMENDMENTS OVER THE YEARS

....

As Tyrone and Monique became more familiar with each other and comfortable in their married life they were able to be more in tune to each other. "I know that I am a blessed man having such a good wife as Monique in my life even though sometimes I don't believe I deserve someone like her." His thoughts were of her as he pulled up into the driveway to their home. It is late and he knows Monique is going to be upset because he did not call to let her know he would be late coming home. The truth is he was really out with the boys but she will never believe him. He knows also that she is a little jealous and thinks he is cheating on her with another woman. "I know I haven't been truthful some times, but never with another woman. My thoughts have been on my wife all night while I was out with the boys. All I was doing was unwinding and having drinks with the boys. Sometimes comfort can be hanging with the boys."

Tyrone took a quick shower and slipped into bed next to Monique. He reached over and pulled her over to him and it was obvious how good it felt. "Monique, I have been thinking about you all night and I couldn't wait to be with you this way." She was humble and enjoyed.

"Monique, oooh aaah Monique I love you." "Shhhh, not during climax time and I'm headed there. Almost immediately after Monique's scream of orgasm there was a short silence, and then like a roll of thunder came a loud bellow from the guts of Tyrone's very soul. There they both lay, just looking at the ceiling and panting like beasts of the wild, only indoors. "Damn, Tyrone, I could hear my name, the Mo and the Nique in clarity and in depth, bouncing off the walls of our bedroom, that scared the shit out of me!"

Two

TEN O'CLOCK A.M. SATURDAY MORNING

....

"Tyrone, what would you like for breakfast this morning?" I know Angel and Ty will most likely have their regular bowl of cereal and fruit." "I will have whatever you're having Sweetheart." "Well my dear husband, I will be having a strong cup of caffeine coffee with an explanation as to your where about and with whom until 3:00 a.m. this morning, how would you like yours served, lying down or sitting up?"

MAKING UP IS SO GOOD

After rain comes sunshine

....

"Baby, I feel so good when you are lying here next to me. I don't know what I would do if the two of us should separate, because I know without a doubt that I would not be able to make it without you in my life. I would simply die. Monique, I could never cheat on you with another woman, and I do not want to ever hurt you. I love you with all my heart, I'm all yours. Lying here next to you lets me know what a blessed man I am to have you as my wife. I feel like I am the luckiest man alive at this moment and I cherish it with all my heart and soul. I thank God for you when I say my prayers at night because baby I need you and I love you and if I ever fail to meet any of your needs, please Monique, just let me know. Here I am lying next to you, looking into your face my dear wife, and with your warm body next to mine, I can smell the soft scent of my favorite perfume on your skin. It makes me want to slow kiss you until I have kissed every inch of your body, like old times before the kids were born, and I can't resist!" ("YA'LL, I FELL FOR IT, HOOK, LINE, AND SINKER.")

IN THE NAME OF LOVE

We cater to our mates

No matter what it takes

We follow their leads

Meeting selfish demanding needs

It takes a strong willing soul

To get from under a controlling hold

And until we learn the difference between a hawk and a dove

We will always cater to the man,

IN THE NAME OF LOVE.

ONE WEEK LATER SATURDAY MORNING, EIGHT O'CLOCK A.M.

....

"Tyrone, wake up, we both have over slept, and I am suppose to meet someone this morning at ten o'clock at my boutique. You may remember the lady who came in one day while you were there about two months ago. As a matter of fact, the two of you hit it off very well in conversation. She got everybody's attention when she walked through the door. She was very well groomed with the looks and the body to show off what she was wearing. Tyrone, don't you remember her? I can't believe I am sitting here waiting for this man to give me a straight civilized answer instead of an off-the-wall, stupid look. This fool is sitting here stuttering when I know that he can out talk our most popular comedian. By the way sweetheart, her name is Samantha."

"What in the hell is going on with this man, pretending he doesn't remember the fancy lady. Whatever it is I'll catch up with it eventually. I like to slow walk down my, sh**. Not that I want to catch him so much, because I can put a detective on it if that is the case. I just want to know how deep he is out there so that I can get my stuff together and put my plans in place so tight he wouldn't know what hit him. I will have all my stuff, all his stuff, and all our stuff sewed up legally in my pocket book tighter than a size small condom on a size large dick. I will have my legal team coming at his ass in ways he never dreamed of. My lawyer husband, better pay attention and know what his wife is capable of doing to a man who wronged her. He will know the power of a mad black woman, and that is the kind of experience no man wants to encounter." Monique is angry in her own thoughts.

"Tyrone, maybe you just don't remember her. I thought that you may have remembered her because of the impact she made when she walked through the door of my boutique that day a couple of months ago. She was noticed by everybody in the place. Sweetheart, I sometime forget that because you are a lawyer, you are constantly around women who present themselves as she did. Tyrone, the reason I brought her up is because she is coming to see me about putting her line of designer clothing in my boutique." "Monique, baby, I am so sorry but I just don't seem to recall her, you can understand that so many people especially women have crossed my path within the past two months."

"I must hurry or I'll be late for the appointment that I have set up with Ms. Samantha Skye. I have exactly two hours to get a cup of caffeine in me, take my shower, get dressed and be at my boutique by ten o'clock this morning. I will stop by one of my favorite quick stop places like Coney Island

Restaurant and pick up a breakfast on the way to my shop. Just thinking about Tyrone, I cannot believe this man of mine pretending that he does not know Samantha. The man talked with the woman for about an hour before she tore herself away from him and walked very quickly out the door. I find it very hard to believe this man, but I have to remember also that I am not a man."

PLAYING DETECTIVE

……………………………...

As Monique drove maximum speed down the John C. Lodge Freeway headed south she had many thoughts running through her mind. Her main thought was on Samantha and Tyrone's stupid actions when confronted about her. "If that woman is playing in my stuff, she's got a sho-nuff-down-home-whipping coming to her ass. After all the hard work I have put into being a good wife to that man, my plan is to keep him not turn him over to some high-heel-stepping-hussy easing her way in and showing off with her social pussy strut….. in other words, her whorish up-to-no-good ass."

Monique comes up off the Lodge Freeway and stopped off at a Coney Island Restaurant and ordered breakfast for her guest and herself, since she didn't have time to eat before leaving home. She didn't want to have Samantha waiting for her which is a bad impression for a boss. Monique thought, I could have called in the breakfast order and it would have been ready for me when I arrived.

A little while later, Monique arrived at her shop and Samantha was already there waiting in her car. "I am sorry I am running behind time this morning, Ms. Skye, have you been waiting long?" "I just arrived about five minutes ago." "I wasn't sure if you had eaten breakfast yet and I know I haven't so I stopped and got some for us. I have a table in the back room where we can eat and take care of our business for today. I will interview you while we eat our breakfast. I will make a pot of coffee to have with our breakfast; I prefer to make my own. I hope you like it strong and with caffeine." "Strong with caffeine is the way I like it Ms. Haywill." Monique smiled at her own wicked thought as she spoke quietly under her breath, "I bet you like your men the same damn way heifer, kicking it strong with the energy of caffeine."

Before Monique started the interview with Samantha she started the conversation about the day she came into the shop. Monique said to Samantha, "you acted as if you knew my husband before you came into my shop." "Your husband! You mean Lacy's friend, Tyrone?" "I think we're on the same page, go on." Mrs. Haywill, Lacy is my man and Tyrone just happened to be a friend of my man. I am so sorry that you had other thoughts about me on your mind." Monique, the woman with all the mouth was without words. "Enough of all this man talk, we got important business to take care of before I open my store for business. After all, today is Saturday, a work free weekend for a woman to shop and spend her man's money." "Girl, you got that right." All the time Monique is thinking, trap time, "and believe me, Ms. Samantha Skye, you're gonna get it, just wait until the time is right and I get together with my best friend Imani, who is your so-call-man's wife."

"Before we get started, let me explain a few things to you. As you already know, the name of my shop is Monique's Boutique. Monique's Boutique carries only name brand top quality clothing and underwear, and we also carry shoes with limited sizes and also purses. I expect you to come up to my specification in quality merchandise if I choose to use your line of clothing. Let's talk contract and money." Samantha soon leaves. Monique feels a little exhausted playing detective and at the same time handles business such as hers, and her thoughts are wondering, "I am so glad this meeting is over."

"It is midday and that man is not answering his phone. I am wondering, what's the matter. Tyrone knows that I am accustomed to our midday contact and I am mentally programmed for him either in person or by phone around this time of day." Since today is Saturday and no court or clients for today, I don't have to put a muzzle on it. All I can say at this time is HEEEE HAAAA, make the noise, make the noise, make the noise. I am ready to close up my boutique for Tyrone. The girls are spending the day with their friends over in Beverly Hills where their father dropped them off before noon. His ass was suppose to go straight back home and relax for the day. Where is he?"

Rrrrring, Rrrrring, Rrrrring, Rrrrring, Rrrrring. "Where can the man be and what is he doing where he can't answer his cell phone. I just can't imagine him using our time of togetherness to be with another woman. And if he keeps telling me that he was out with the boys, then I am going to start wondering about that too. Right now I need answers, and when I close shop and go home he better be there." Rrrring, Rrrring, "Monique's Boutique, may I help---Tyrone where have you been? I have been trying to reach you for the past hour, and you better not tell me you were out with the boys when you're supposed to be at home resting and waiting for me to return. What is your explanation, now start explaining. Tyrone, I know you are not stuttering to me on the phone, what is the matter with you? I know your work can get you down sometimes, but sweetheart, you know that I am with you all the way, with all that you need me to do to help you. Tyrone, I think we need to have a serious talk. I'm on my way home. I am with you through thick and thin. I know we have trust in each other and now we need to talk. I mean sit down with each other and have a good husband and wife talk. I am not talking about another woman I think you might have been with, I am talking about helping my husband work through problems that maybe, the outside people do not need to know about, whatever the issues might be. Sweetheart, it will be just you and me." Tyrone responded very sweetly, "thanks, baby." "Tyrone, before I hang up I want to say I'm sorry for the way I came on to you

on the phone, and please remember that you know how high strung I can get and how bent out of shape I get when things don't go as I expect them to."
"Monique Just hurry home."

Three

AT THE BALL MANSION
(Imani is on cloud nine)

Rrrrring, rrrrring, rrrrring, rrrrring, rrrrring, rrrrring, rrrrring, rrrrring, rrrrring---click. "Well, I guess Monique is out running errands early this morning before those Saturday shoppers start coming in. I will try her on her cell phone later and, give her the good news about my transcript being printed into book form. I want the two of us to have a special one on one celebration, and, the big celebration will come when Lacy throws the big party that he promised for what he calls the # 1 best, seller for me the third time around. I know he and Tyrone will put their heads together to make it a spectacular occasion and of course the two men will call on and depend on Monique to make it happen. I know she will make sure the beauty shop crowd will be there because they are good people and they know how to make a party jump. I am a happy woman and I feel so blessed."

"Imani, sweetheart, your happiness makes you look even more beautiful than you already are." "Lacy, you look very excited yourself, this book is affecting both of us, and it feels good." "I have been trying to reach Monique with no success. I can't wait to see her and tell her the exciting news before it becomes public news. Since it is time for us two ladies to meet for lunch and have our girlfriend talk and catch up on the things we've been doing, of course the bragging will be more than about our husbands and our children, this time I got bragger's rights. By the way, Lacy, do you and Tyrone ever discuss your wives, Imani and Monique when you guys get together with what you call hanging out with your boys?" "Ha, ha, ha, Imani, you will not get me there. Our boys have a code of honor that goes without word sayings and that is what make boys night out exactly what it says which is, boys night out." "Mmmmm, just give it a little time and I will break that damn code."

Imani called Monique's cell phone and Monique answered right away. "Hello, Monique, girl where have you been? I called you at work and there was no answer and no, I did not leave a message. Girlfriend, this is more than a message kind of phone call and we need to get together right away. I got good news I can barely hold and I need to tell you first. What are you doing within the next hour?" "Nothing, I'm all yours, what's next? "That was a lie but she is my best friend and she needs me for just a short time span, I hope." "Can you come over, Lacy is just leaving. He is going to the office late today. He said, that he is meeting a client there which is highly unusual because today is Saturday, his off day. I didn't ask questions because I didn't want to upset him. The man seems to be on edge all the time but I know he loves me and he does support me in my writing, as a matter of fact, he critiques my transcripts for me. Girl, I am so excited and we got some things to talk about so come on over. Don't eat anything because I am putting together a light brunch for us, you just come on, I'll be waiting for you."

AN EXCITING DAY FOR IMANI

(Her best friend by her side)

....

By the time Monique arrived at the Ball mansion, Imani had everything ready and set out in a fashionable manner. "Imani, it looks like you are ready to celebrate something that is big time. What's going on?" Monique, as soon as we start eating I will start talking." "Girl your whole body is bubbling over, you had better start talking now, and I am ready to listen."

"Monique, look at me." "Ok, I'm looking, what is it that I am supposed to see?" "You are looking at the person whose publisher just released her third book. My publisher said she believes it will become a #1 best seller and this is what I have been working so hard toward. This is my third #1 best seller and I feel good about it. I have used my gift for writing and I feel that I am being blessed over and over again. My readers are my reward and I thank my Heavenly Father for letting me make it all happen. Now that the book is in print, I am ready to celebrate. That is where you come in and help make it a party to remember." "You know that's a done deal, don't worry about a thing. I think you already know that your husband has to call me first. We know about that man thing and being in charge which means giving orders and making everything magically happen without the fuss, ha, ha, ha."

"Imani, I want you to know right now that I do not want you to give me a copy of your book as a gift because I want to be the one to buy your first copy and have you sign it. Excuse me while I make my order for my book." "Monique, I feel like I'm on cloud nine and I never want to come down. As a matter of fact, I think this call for a toast, don't you?" "It's a bit early for that, don't you think?" "Monique, I know it's early, but I do think a bottle of champagne is in order for this occasion, don't you think so? It should go well with our brunch since I added steak as one of the meats and I did not forget your toasted crab cakes and thick grits with a side of egg omelets." "Imani, we started talking and never bothered to look at the food, and I know you put a lot of work into it. Do I smell blueberry muffins? I am ready to eat, and I may taste everything you have laid out. First, let's toast to your book, that comes first, and then we can pig out. Imani, I am so happy for you and I bet Lacy feels like a lucky man, having a wife who is beautiful and gifted."

"Monique, I don't know what I would do without you. I know that I can always count on you and I know that you always got my back. Dear friend, it just occurred to me that you are a part of my happiness, you are my best friend and that is why sharing the joy of my book with you is so important to me." "I would be mad as hell if you didn't make me a part of the celebration. I am going to have fun planning this party with Lacy." Monique is thinking, "maybe it will give me a chance to find out more about what is going on with him and that damn Samantha Skye."

"Oh, look at the time, I'm sorry Imani but I got to run. I told Tyrone that I was on my way home and he's suppose to be there waiting for me. He is waiting for me so that we can iron out a few things. I enjoyed discussing and being a part of the celebration and I know Tyrone will be excited too, but right now he is trying to iron out something that he needs to include his wife in. Once that is done, we both can relax and enjoy what we call pure sex." Girl, get out of here and take care of your business.

I just wish it was me. Tyrone is still tired all the time and I am being neglected big time in that area. Get out of here now, I'll talk with you later." "Imani, I will call you tomorrow and we can meet somewhere for lunch and talk some more, bye, bye." "Bye."

"Poor Imani, she has no idea that she and her husband along with that Samantha will be a part of my discussion with Tyrone. After the meeting with Samantha at my boutique this morning, I see nothing but drama in the Ball family future. I will play it by ear as to which direction Tyrone and I will go with two subjects on the table. I have my husband to think about and I have my best friend to think about. I have a lot on my plate."

LORDY, LORDY, LET ME LIVE TO BE FORTY!
(Too much on Monique's plate)

Monique has things coming up in her future she had not planned on, but caught in the middle of other people's drama and her thoughts are occupied in the mess big time. "Samantha Skye is up to no good. I can feel it, and I also believe that she knows Lacy Ball is a married man. Anything that affects Imani may very well affect me since I'm her best friend and I care about what happens to her. I hope this will blow over because I have so much on my plate at this time, and I don't need added drama to the pile."

As Monique heads home, she is hoping that Tyrone will be there when she gets home. She was leaving her shop when Imani phoned her to come over and the urgency in her voice made her go there instead of straight home to Tyrone, who is suppose to be at home waiting for her. This is going to be a long day, but the good part is getting home to spend time with her husband. She thought that she would already be at home to join him as planned for today.

Monique felt relieved when she arrived home and Tyrone's car was in the driveway. She sat for a moment as she mumbles under breath, "his damn ass had better been at home. Today is Saturday so I say, damn his boys, hell, I'm his wife." As she got out of her car, and walked hurriedly up to her front entrance and opened the door, she saw no movement through the glass doors leading into the main entrance of the house. Suddenly, Tyrone appeared with both arms extended waiting for her with a smile on his face. For Monique, that was an instant body wrap and she walked into them and stood there motionless enjoying his warm caressing muscular arms around her.

Monique wanted to start her and Tyrone's day together with good news so once they went to their place of comfort in the house she begin to tell him about Imani's good news. "Baby I am happy about Imani's new book and I hope this book becomes a #1best seller for her. I bet Lacy is walking on clouds with her." "Sweetheart, I think it is about time for us to talk about your best friend, Lacy Ball. By the way, did you eat yet?" "No I have not eaten yet, have you?" "While I was at Imani's house, I had brunch which she set up for my visit with her. She knew that I would come running when I heard the urgency in her voice when she phoned me. I apologize for being late coming home when I told you that I would be coming home straight from my shop after my meeting with Ms. Samantha Skye. Before we talk, I am going to prepare a nice lunch for you. How about a big juicy roast beef sandwich with the works and Caesar salad with a few grape leaves mixed in, and to go with it I will serve ice tea and a slice of chocolate cake, how does that sound?" "As always, you got it going on, and all I got to do is enjoy." "That's what I'm talking about, APPRECIATION."

PROBLEMS IN OUR TIGHT CIRCLE

"Tyrone, I want to start our talk by saying again that I am sorry about coming down so hard on you, acting like a jealous woman, and second, I want to say that I am so in love with you. As my husband, I love you, but it goes deeper than that. What I am trying to tell you, Tyrone is that you have captured me, not just in body but in mind and soul and when I look at myself I see you. I had not thought about us that way until Imani said something to me concerning Lacy. I know that she wants to talk to me about her problem, but I have been avoiding it and after my conversation with Samantha this morning, I think it is a serious problem and I also know who the problem is.

"Monique, we have a few hours before we have to pick the kids up from their friend's house. We can get comfortable and relax while we talk. Baby, you know I must remind you that if Lacy doesn't involve me in this situation, I will not interfere where he is concern. He has to call on me if he wants my input in his love life. I'm sorry, Monique, but this is the way I feel about it and this is the way it's going to be. I love you but that is a line I refuse to cross. Why don't we strip out of these street clothes and get comfortable now, before another word is said."

As Monique turns over in her mind what she wants to say about Ms Samantha, her whole body becomes tense, when suddenly without warning----- "That damn husband snatcher is about to get kicked back to where the hell she came from if she thinks she's gonna move in on my friend, Imani with Lacy." "Baby, what are you talking about? Do you need to back up and start all over again? It looks like you have put the buggy before the mule from where I stand." "Well, sit down and let me do the talking because I got everything straight from the horse's mouth."

"A few of weeks ago while having lunch with Imani, she told me that Lacy was coming home from work late every night. She said that he has not touched her in weeks. That is not all she had to say about that man, she also said that his excuse is always the same, "Imani, I am just too tired to engage in that kind of activity." "Imani said Lacy would turn over facing opposite direction from her and fall fast asleep. I don't know why the hell she let him wake up, he's already lying there dead to her needs, just help the man rest in peace (RIP)." "Monique, that is cold." "Cold my ass, so why don't you put it to the test. Man, you know when I lay there next to you and open my legs I am ready, and you have never missed picking up on that."

"Tyrone, let's move forward. I got plenty to say concerning that Ms. Samantha Skye. As you know, I had a meeting with her this morning about putting her line of clothing in my boutique. After talking with her, I don't want that woman nowhere near my place of business. That she-dog had the nerve to say to me that you, my dear husband, is the friend of her man, Lacy Ball. What do you have to say about that, Tyrone?" "It all seems one sided to me Monique. You're just guessing and Lacy hasn't said anything yet, and as long as he is silent on the subject there is no proof. Some women jump to the wrong conclusion about men and sexual activity with them. Like I said, Monique, if Lacy wants my input he would ask me for it." "Tyrone, I am not about to argue with you about something you have more experience in than me. Damn, I have no experience in it so I will listen to the man, he just might be right."

"Monique, all this drama with Imani and Lacy has made me forget about my own situation, which I can see now, is just plain petty stuff." "Tyrone, we still need to talk, and remember that my shoulder is here for you to cry on whenever you need to." "Baby, what I saw as a mountain is now a mole hill in comparison to my problem and I personally feel much better where I am concerned. I have had so many things going on with personal problems and, with my head wondering in so many different directions, I don't know how to begin to talk to you about me. I think our best friends might be calling on us for comfort, if things are as bad as you say, so I'll just put my little thing on hold to pick up later if it's okay with you." "Fine with me, I won't argue about it."

"Tyrone, I am so happy that we are now on the same page where Imani and Lacy is concerned. I always knew that Imani was happy in her marriage and for her to be such a happy, and pleasant person, I know things were good at home. Sometimes I would say certain things to her and she would giggle like a high school girl in love. Tyrone I know you remember when we all use to spend most of our weekends together and the four of us had so much fun in whatever we did. Imani was always full of laughs and Lacy couldn't take his eyes off her. I know they were very much in love."

"Monique, like always, you hit the nail on the head. There was no problems in Imani's and Lacy's marriage until Samantha came on the scene and I'm still hoping that we're guessing. It's hard for me to believe that Lacy would be so obvious as to neglect his wife with no regard to her feelings what so ever. It's not like Lacy to hurt anyone on purpose. Monique I just don't get it." "Tyrone, I have faith with my actions, just follow my lead for a change." "Oh well, what the heck, you just may be right."

Monique is up bright and early in the morning and the first thing that came to mind was to call Imani and see if she can come by this morning after dropping Angel and Ty, Jr. off to school. She feels like bonding with her friend today and uplifting her spirits. Monique heard Tyrone moving around and decided to throw the idea at him.

"Good morning sweetheart, did you sleep well last night?" "Why do you ask, did I toss and turn in my sleep last night?" "My my why are you so grouchy this morning? You did not toss and turn in your sleep last night and if you're upset with me, I am sorry but I really was too tired. Tyrone sweetheart, I do plan to double your pleasure tonight, it's planned so expect it."

"Tyrone I need to ask you a question." "What is it now, Monique, I mean honey." "Yeah, right, anyway, what do you think about me calling Imani this morning and paying her a visit just to talk and cheer her up if she needs it?" "I think it's a great idea. I'm sure she will enjoy having you over." "I'll call her now and see if it's okay if I stop by after dropping thc kids off at school this morning."

Rrrrrring rrrrrring rrrrrring rrrrrring, "hello"…."hello Imani, I know it's early for me to be calling but I would like to stop by for a little while this morning for us to chat and have coffee together. I will bring something to go along with the coffee. Is it okay for me to stop by girlfriend?" "Monique, you know you're welcome at my house anytime you feel like stopping by. I look forward to seeing you and I will have the coffee perked and waiting. I also have yogurt and mixed fruit to serve with the coffee, bye….click.

"Thank goodness it's Friday." Monique caught herself mumbling again. She opens her shop late in the day on Fridays because she opens extra early on Saturdays. She plans to spend at least an hour with Imani and run a couple of errands before opening her boutique today. What Monique really wants from her visit with Imani is for Imani to initiate a conversation about, Lacy and herself with the topic centered around, neglect. Monique thinks that once Imani is no longer in denial concerning Lacy's treatment of her, everything will come to a head and then she and the damn fool will have to deal with, it. What Imani needs to do is put a foot in the low down heifer's ass and bake that cheating Lacy a sweet potato pie.

Ding Dong ding dong, "good morning Monique, come on in, I can see you brought breakfast with you." "I have two breakfast orders here and I hope you're hungry." "I am hungry for food and I am hungry for adult company." "Imani, I thought two adults lived in this house, did one of them move out?" "Lacy might as well not be living here because he comes home late and he leaves here early every morning for work. My husband has changed and I don't know why, but I don't want to bore you with this, so let's change the subject to something pleasant." "Bore me bore me, please bore me, if you have a problem, I have a problem. Imani, I am not going to make you talk to me right now, but we will get together and talk about your problem, and that damn fool you call a husband."

Four

It is Monday morning and Tyrone arrives at his office early. While looking over notes left on his desk by his secretary, he ponders over all that took place over the weekend. He decided not to mention to Lacy the conversation his wife Monique had with Samantha Skye at Monique's Boutique on Saturday morning. It wasn't long before he heard moving around in the outer office. "Good morning, Attorney Haywill." "Good morning, Cheryl, will you please let me know when Attorney Ball comes in." "I will Sir, and I will have your coffee ready right away sir." After two cups of coffee Tyrone was wide awake with plenty energy. "Cheryl, since

I have, two cases today in court I will not be coming back to the office today, and also alert the young lady who comes in as your part time help with records to put my messages in urgency order."

Tyrone had already left for court before Lacy got to the office and it seems lately that they have been missing each other, especially around lunchtime where they usually meet up between court schedules. Tyrone made a quick phone call and smiled as he said goodbye and hung up. As soon as court was over he rushed from the building as if he was in a hurry to be somewhere.

Rrrring, rrrring, rrrring, rrrring, rrrring---click. Monique hangs up the phone in an angry manner. "Tyrone is not answering his phone but I will call him again in a few minutes before I jump to a conclusion." This is not a happy day for Monique, and it shows clearly on her face. Not even her expensive makeup can hide that fact. "I will check with Imani and see how she is handling things. We may need to talk before my dinner party and also before her celebration for her newly published book."

Rrrring, rrrring, rrrring, "hello, the Ball resident, how may I help you?" "Imani, this is Monique, I'm just calling to see how you're doing today. I was thinking about you and I want to know is Lacy still acting like a damn fool? He has to know that you're worried about him coming home late every night." Monique I'm sorry that I brought my problem to you, will you please forget about it. I should not have said anything to you about what is happening with me and Lacy. I am on my way over to Brown Sugar Beauty Salon to pay visit to our friend Ms. B." "That big mouth woman is your friend not mine, she is just a hang on because of you. Anyway, you can tell Ms. B I said hello." "Monique, we will talk later if that is okay with you." That's fine with me, call me when you're free for us to talk, goodbye." "Bye, Monique.

"I think it is time for me to call that husband of mine again. I can't understand why I keep having strange feelings concerning Tyrone after all; he has been a good husband to me." Rrrring, rrrring--- "Monique, I was about to call you. I saw where you have been trying to reach me, and baby, I'm sorry about not calling you back right away, but I was tied up in court." Tyrone was tied up alright, but not in the courtroom, but where he always spends his time when Monique can't reach him. "Tyrone, since you're finished with your court cases, I want you to please come home so you can relax and clear your mind by talking to me and I will do nothing but listen and speak only if you want me to. How does that sound sweetheart?" That sounds fine to me, I'll see you in a couple of hours, I need to stop off at my office first." "I'll see you in a couple of hours, bye sweetheart." "Bye, Monique." Monique went home and Tyrone joined her later, a little late but he did come home.

"Tyrone, I knew once I got you home early and I got you in the shower and relaxed your body with a lengthy body massage that you would feel better with a rested mind." "Baby it took the stress away." "Tyrone, I don't want you to talk or think about anything for the next hour. I just want you to sit here in your comfortable chair and listen to some of your classical jazz. It always helps you to relax. I will be back in a moment with a glass of chilled wine." "Monique, you're so good to me and I can't help but love you. You know it is not always possible for a man to have a beautiful wife who is also kind and generous and true to her man. You're the kind of woman a good man is looking for." "Lucky for you I'm already taken by you." As Monique approached Tyrone with a glass of wine she stuck the tip of her tongue in the wine and bent down to him and touched his lips with her tongue. She could see Mr. Jones rising.

"Sweetheart, it is not the time for us to get busy that way. I am going to the kitchen to prepare a quick lunch for us. And after we have finished eating our lunch we can lie down and relax together; and baby since it is still early and the kids are still in school, I am gonna make you scream so loud that anybody coming near this house will think that I am killing your ass."

"It's been a little while since I've heard my name screamed out so loud that the sound carried throughout the entire house." Tyrone just smiled while thinking, "what a beautiful day this is, like chocolate, double dipped. How long will I be able to live this double life, it scares me sometimes." It seems like Tyrone has a secret life that he is not willing to share with nobody, and he is not willing to do anything that would change his home life with Monique. "I can't imagine not being able to talk to and make love to Monique and be with her the way that I am accustomed to. I love everything about my wife and I am not willing to live without her. As a matter of fact, I am preparing myself to make love to Monique in a way that she is not expecting today. I also know there's that chance for me to reach the ultimate release and ball up like a baby in tears."

"Tyrone has no idea what's in store for him after lunch. Don't think it is just one sided in our bedroom my dear readers. If you came anywhere near our bedroom, you would actually think that the man was whipping my ass. You will hear a lot of moaning and groaning with some screaming when he is hitting it where it needs to be hit. Tyrone and I are two of a same kind and we know it. Ha, ha, ha, ha, sometimes I catch myself laughing about us, especially about things we have done over the years. Like I said, same kind, yes we are."

THE ALMIGHTY TRUTH

…………………………………

"I know that if I ever found out that Tyrone was sleeping with another woman I would have to leave him. Not that I would want to, but because the trust we have with each other would be broken. It would be hard for me to give all of myself to someone who I can't trust. My time and energy is too precious to be wasted on a man who does not appreciate my love and devotion to him. I do hold truth to my husband, to honor him and love him just as it was spoken on the day God joined us together as one in Holy Matrimony. I would never allow another man to put his flesh inside my body while I am married to Tyrone, and I hope Tyrone would never allow his flesh to go inside another woman. I would be hurt to know that I have taken in the evil spirits of sinful women with whom my husband has screwed, or some innocent woman who he lied to or tricked into an affair that she thought was innocent before it was too late to turn back. Some of these women are looking for husbands not realizing the dog in man is at play. Men with loving families are going to keep it that way and they need that stability because it makes them feel worthy of something good. It is sad to say, but the truth is, where there is a will, the dog in man will find a way. Nothing has changed about man and sex since the beginning of time."

SETTING THE MOOD TO TALK WITH TYRONE ABOUT US

....

"Sweetheart, I will be getting up in a few minutes to pick the kids up from school. I want you to stay in bed and rest a little longer and when I get back I will call our favorite family restaurant and make reservation for the family for dinner. When we get back home tonight, I will get Angel and Ty, Jr. off to bed early so that we will be able to talk without interruptions. I just want to give you a chance to clear your mind about whatever it is that is worrying you. Whatever it is that is upsetting to you, I want you to remember that I am your wife and I will be here for you no matter what and how long it takes, as long as it is not about another woman. Everything else I think I can handle." "Monique, I promise you, it is not about another woman, I truly love you."

"Tyrone you have been very quiet for the whole ride here to the restaurant. Let's try to enjoy this evening out with the kids. Wow! Look at what they have done with the parking lot. Hey, look at the beautiful lighted water foundation at the front entrance of the building! I can't wait to see the inside, let's go in everybody." As the Haywill family enters the restaurant and to Monique's surprise there was a big change. "Sweetheart it's been awhile since our last visit to this restaurant. A lot has changed with the décor, and even the music has changed. They have gone from "Bach" to "contemporary jazz", and I love it."

"Tyrone, will you look at who is sitting across the room in front of us, it's Imani and Lacy. Why don't you go over and ask them to join us at our table, we can ask the waiter to bring two more chairs to our table. Angel and Ty, Jr. you wouldn't mind your dad and I inviting our dear friends to join us for dinner would you? I am so happy to see them, aren't you too, Tyrone? The kids don't mind them joining us; please invite them to join us at our table. They don't know that we are here because they have not looked in this direction since we came in, otherwise Imani would have acknowledged us."

Tyrone did just as Monique had asked and the couple was delighted to join their best friends for dinner. After all, they are the kid's god mom and god dad.

"Imani, I am so happy to see you. I have been thinking about you and planning to call you, but other things would always get in my way and I have let all my busy work get in the way of me keeping in touch with my dear best friend. However, I am sure you already know about the upcoming event Tyrone and I are having at our home from your husband. Anyway, Tyrone and I are having a few friends over this coming Saturday for late evening cocktails and light dinner and entertainment. Girlfriend, we got to get our sorority strut together because you know the guys will have their stepping going on and we want to work it too. I do want to see you and Lacy there and I don't want to hear excuses why you can't come. As a matter of fact, I want you to bring your twin girls, Stacey and Lacey prepared to stay overnight at my home. Angel and Ty Jr. always enjoy their company. It will also give us a chance to catch up on what's going on in our lives since we last spent time together."

"Monique I look forward to us get together so I can hear what has been happening since we last saw each other, and I need to talk to you about things I have not been comfortable talking to anyone else about. We can talk with each other because we have a special kind of bonding and love for each other as friends." Monique already knows what it is all about. She suspected something was wrong the last time they met for lunch. She knows that is the reason Imani has been making excuses about lunch for the last few weeks. "I promise you I will call within the next week."

"Ty, Jr. and Angel, don't you want to tell your god mom and god dad about what you have been doing in school? Ty, Jr. why don't you tell them about your science project that ended up a comedy act. Now that was funny. Angel why don't you tell them about your song and dance number that got you a standing ovation." "Ty, Jr. and Angel I promise you that your god dad and I will not miss another one of your programs unless it is absolutely not under our control. I am so sorry we were not there to cheer you on." There was suddenly silence as the waiter stopped at their table and to serve dinner rolls and water before taking their menu orders. That gave everybody a chance to sit back and relax before the waiter came back with the food. It wasn't long before Ty, Jr. blurted out, "with all this good food in front of us smelling so good, I say let's eat."

Five

“Tyrone, will you please stay at home today so that we can talk.” This is more important than I think you realize. Three people’s lives are at stake.” I got his undivided attention. “Yes, sweetheart, three people, count them, 1-2-3, Lacy, Imani, and Samantha. Need I say more?”

“Tyrone you can stop pretending that you don’t know anything about what is going on. Samantha already told me about her and Lacy. When Imani finds out about Lacy's affair, you and I both know it will shatter her life. Marital affairs always have a way of coming from the dark side into the light. Tyrone, you had better talk to Lacy because this is just the beginning of and the making of what we call all hell breaking loose. He needs to talk to Imani, and if he thinks that I am going to sit by and watch my best friend be torn apart just because of the freaky dog in him, he had better think again. I am telling you straight up Tyrone, my friend Imani will not be the loser in Lacy's love games. A man who is too selfish or too weak to walk away from a marriage he doesn't want any more is not really a real man anyway, unless he wants to have his cake and eat it too. I can guarantee you, Imani will not go down without a good fight, and I am on Imani's side, and you better not be on nobody's side who is in the wrong." Tyrone's face instantly changed to a serious expression. "Woman, you listen to me and you listen to me now!" "Tyrone wh…" "Shut up! You will not interfere in Lacy's and Imani's marriage, if Lacy wants me to know what is happening in his life he will tell me. I don't ask because I don't want to know and I don't give a damn. It is his life so let him handle it. Imani knows when it is time for her to walk. The woman is not stupid and she doesn't have to stay and accept his crap."

"Since I have already told Imani about our Saturday evening cocktail party, I expect to see both Imani and Lacy here for the occasion. They are such a beautiful couple and I hate to see them separate over such a thing as infidelity. As bad as it is, as well as hurtful, when one partner is cheating on the other whether it's the woman or the man, a marriage is too important to not at least try to work things out. Those two must remember that it is their children who will be hurt the most through a divorce. And if the love is still there, then there is a chance to talk and work on the problem. Sometimes a good understanding is all that is needed to get a marriage back on track. Whatever the hell he is seeking he can find it right there at home with Imani."

"Are you listening to me, Tyrone?" "Yes, sweetheart, I am listening to every word you're saying." "Tyrone, what Lacy really needs to do is get into the "Word" and take to heart the true meaning of Holy Matrimony. If he honored his marriage as it is stated in the Bible to carry over into his life, he should know that he can't get to Heaven with a mistress and a wife. Lacy Ball should know that he won't get to Heaven with a mistress and a wife. Maybe that cheating man doesn't know that Satan is real and is working hard on his behalf. Also, what Lacy doesn't know is that Jesus is in his household with protection around his wife and children and the power of prayer is strong and will win over evil all the way, all the time. He better pay attention." "You better stay out of it."

CHEATERS

For whatever reason

Throughout any season

Temptation comes in creeping

Seeking lust with lowdown sneaking

The demons are busy at play

And it's all good Satan's way

So don't get caught in the mix

You know when it's the devil's fix

Sex and money is what he will use

And sooner or later you will pay your dues

So whatever is on your deceitful, dirty mind

Your mate and your bedroom can mesh in divine

So please, for your children, try to be leaders

And not the parents who are

CHEATERS

"Tyrone, I know it may be easy to get caught up in a love triangle, and I also know the triangle is with that third person who allowed herself to get involved with a married man. Samantha can always walk away and never look back, but Lacy is married with family and will always be connected to his children and also connected to his wife even if they're not together, but through their children. There will always be bittersweet memories for the rest of their lives. Tyrone I pray that I never have to live without you while we both are still above the ground. Now, if I ever catch you cheating on me and giving my stuff to someone else, I may have to walk, but not until after I have eliminated or tried to eliminate your black ass."

HEART TO HEART SERIOUS TALK

....

"Tyrone, I am so happy the two of us can sit down and have a serious talk and share our concerns about our friends' well being." "Monique, you have to remember that Lacy is not just a friend, he is my best friend. I will do whatever needs to be done within my power to help my best friend. What I will not do is interfere where I am not wanted. The minute Lacy tells me to back off, I am gone. I cannot make a grown man do what he doesn't want to do and I will not jeopardize our longtime friendship over bullshit concerning some woman who is most likely giving the man what he is afraid to ask his wife for. If there is something more he needs, then there is something more that his wife may want or needs while getting and delivering pleasure."

"I believe our best friends have a chance to make a recovery from this ordeal." "I know I'll be happy, and you, Tyrone, will be happy, and to hell with women of the streets. Let them find somebody else's stupid husbands to devour. Yes, I said stupid and that does not leave Lacy out. When he cannot control his flesh, then he is stupid and weak. Thank goodness it's not their next door neighbor, otherwise Imani and Lacy would have to move."

To keep his own sanity and peace at home, Tyrone decided to go along with Monique and have Lacy and Imani over so that the four of them can sit down and talk about what is going on concerning Samantha Skye and her actualization about Lacy and herself. The honest truth is, the whole thing is nothing new to Tyrone except the part about the conversation between Monique and Samantha. Tyrone never liked what Lacy was doing but not even he could have stopped a grown man from acting a fool to satisfy the flesh. I can't help him and I defiantly can't let the mess spill over into my life and cause trouble in my household. My family is important to me and the love of my life and I don't want to lose that. Lacy's affair with Samantha should have been their deep dark secret.

"Baby, when do you think is a good time for Lacy and Imani to come over so we can sit down and talk? I was thinking maybe the weekend after our cocktail party. Meanwhile I will talk with Lacy at the office when we have a little free time between court cases and clients coming in for appointments." "Sweetheart, I will talk with Imani within the next two days. It is about time for us to have our girly talk and catch up on all the good news, and what is happening with that out-crowd of whom she socializes with sometimes." "Please, dear Lord, as I have you in my thoughts this moment, put it on my heart to find the right words to say to my friend, Imani. I know it is a critical area to go into, but I do feel that it must be done. I believe it should be done by someone who cares about her and will be there for her in time of need, and with a shoulder to cry on for as long as needed. I ask of this in your son, Jesus, name, amen."

Rrrrring, Rrrrring, Rrrrring, "hello---Monique, I was just about to call you. Girl, it is about time for us to get together and talk. I want to catch up on what is happening with that out-crowd you hang with sometimes. I am talking about Ms. B and the ladies from her Beauty Shop. Does she still think that she is the finest thing living in Detroit, Michigan? I don't know who lead her to believe that lie, ha, ha, ha." "Monique, you will never change, and you better not change because I love you this way. The girls at the shop miss you. They have not seen you since your last big fashion show. Ms. B told me the next time I see you to tell you to come in and get those locks tightened. She still talk about the time you decided to lock. She calls your locks dreadlocks because you dreaded the decision after putting so much money into it and then you had a change of mind. You finally became comfortable with your new style especially after you realized it is more than just a style. We all say you made a wise decision because it looks beautiful on you and you wear it with pure essence of a strong black woman. When shall I tell the girls that you will be coming in to a visit with your so-call pals at Ms. B's Beauty Shop? You know Ms. B will have your favorite Champagne on hand.

"Monique, I am free for tomorrow if that is a good time for the two of us." "Imani, if you want we can have lunch at my shop. I'll call a Chinese Restaurant and put together a nice lunch for us. I remember all your favorites in Chinese foods, and my shop will be the perfect place since we will be at a place with no interruptions cutting into our flow of conversation and we do not have to whisper, just eat and talk." "Okay, but let's not forget about a future visit to Ms. B's, Brown Sugar's Beauty Shop."

BEING A BEST FRIEND

....

Imani arrives at Monique's boutique shop feeling good about spending time one on one with her best friend without their husbands being nearby in the same place doing what business men usually do, **TALK BUSINESS**! She calls Monique on her cell phone. "Hey girl, Imani, I'm here, my hands are full. Girl, I brought us something to celebrate with." Imani gets out of her car with two bottles of champagne and two champagne glasses. Monique rushed to the door and opened it wide not knowing what to expect. As Imani walks in she is taken aback by the sight of so much food. Monique bought both her and Imani's favorite foods from the Chinese Restaurant. "Monique, what in the world are we going to do with all this food?" "We eat some and take some home to our husbands. My kids will be having pizza and salad for dinner and if hubby doesn't want Chinese food he too can have pizza." As Imani looks around, "Girlfriend, every time I come into your shop, you have done something more fantastic in the place. Just tell me where to put the champagne bottles, they need to stay cold, where is your ice bucket? I can see you already have the table set up for lunch and it looks nice."

"Imani, it is so nice to have you here. I didn't ask you here for girl talk, as a matter of fact, I ask you to come here to talk with you about something very important. It is time for us to talk man talk, and to make it specific, husband talk." "Monique what are you talking about, is my husband in some kind of trouble?" Imani, I think you've been expecting this talk, and you know you've been edging it on in conversation with me, first at Fishbone Restaurant and again at your home."

"I think it's about time we talk about what's on both our minds, I will go first." "There is a woman who I want to talk to you about and that is why I had you to come here today. Her name is Samantha

Skye, does that ring a bell with you? "A woman came into the beauty shop yesterday while I was there, I think she did introduce herself as Samantha Skye, but what does she have to do with me, and you better not say she is a long lost cousin of mine?" "Not that close but she has her eyes on your man. Now before you say a word, let me tell you about Samantha and Lacy." "Start talking and you better know what you are talking about because it is hard for me to believe that Lacy has been cheating on me with another woman." "All I know is that Samantha came into my boutique one evening and engaged in a long conversation with my husband. I thought it was strange that they didn't seem strangers to each other. After almost an hour talking with Tyrone she walked hurriedly out the door. Tyrone told me a couple of days ago that he did not remember Samantha or ever talking to her." "But what does Tyrone and Samantha talking with each other, have to do with me?" "Imani, will you please stop interrupting me so that I can tell you exactly what is going on! Please no more interruptions."

"A few days ago, Ms. Samantha Skye came into my boutique and she asked me to allow her to show her one of a kind personal clothing line. I looked through the book and I liked what I saw. We talked about her clothes and I then set up an appointment with her at my store a couple of days ago. During our conversation I mentioned her and Tyrone's long conversation on the day she dropped by my boutique about a month ago. To my surprise she said that she was surprised to see Tyrone there and asked me, who was he to me. I told her that Tyrone was a fixture around here. I then asked her how did she know Tyrone, and that is when she said he was a friend of her friend, Lacy. Of course I talked with Tyrone about it and he suggested and approved that I talk with you about this, so here we are. I know the two of you can work things out and don't forget about those beautiful twin girls you need to raise together. I'm sure trying to work through a failing marriage might be rough but it can work out and in your case it will work because girlfriend you are going to fight for your man and your marriage. The two of you can build from this point as a beginning of something new and good. Be mad as hell if you must but please think about it. Tyrone will be talking to Lacy sometime this week, maybe tomorrow.

"Monique, I thank you for your advice. I can assure you that nothing is happening between me and Lacy that I can't handle. I am no fool and I can tell you that whatever is happening is nothing I could have done short of busting a cap in somebody's ass, which I have thought about many times. I chose prayer over murder."

"Imani, please don't throw away your marriage out of anger. I know it must hurt, but time has a way of healing deep wounds." "Monique, I have something I need to talk with you about. I have wanted to talk with you for a long time about this; but I have been too afraid, and if it ever got out my life would be shattered. Please hear me out. I just want you to listen---no talking, please." "But

Imani"---"Damn-it Monique, I said no talking, one more word and I am out of here, and I mean it!" "Ok, Imani, there will be no more talking from me, I promise you." Monique saw the angry look on Imani's face and she realized that this must be a serious matter that called for her attention with no feedback from her. She quietly awaited the next move or word from Imani without a mumbling word from her.

Six

COMING OUT OF THE CLOSET

....

Imani begins to tell her deep dark secret to Monique and it is something that Monique would not have had a clue, not in a million years. It is something a person will not randomly guess at. "Monique, although we have been friends for a long time, I could never find the right time to tell you about this secret that I have been keeping from you. Do you remember the time you came into the beauty shop and walked straight to the back without making yourself heard, and you saw Ms. B and me with our arms around each other and I told you she was having man trouble? Well my best friend, to wrap the whole story up in a nutshell, and just be straight with you about me, is that Ms. B and I are together, we are lovers. I have known all along that my husband was having an affair because he was not keeping me sexually satisfied as a wife should be. He would come home pretending that he is tired and let me lay there next to him untouched all night long. Laying there night after night next to my husband I felt the pain and each night it cut deeper and deeper and it hurt like hell. I can tell you, hurting love just ain't worth the pain. Because he is your husband's best friend, I decided not to get you involved. Now that you know, I expect you to tell Tyrone because keeping secrets like this could cause problems in your marriage."

"Monique, I want you to know that I appreciate you for looking out for me and not wanting my husband to mess over me. You are truly my best friend for trying to cushion the blow, and I love you for being here for me. Now you can speak, and for heaven sake, please pull your jaws together." "Uh, uh, uh, damn-it, I am just speechless!"

TO SHARE THIS SECRET WITH MY HUSBAND OR NOT

"Lord let me drive with a steady hand. This decision I must make has to be the perfect one because it could destroy my best friend's marriage. A man knows how to compete with another man, but if it's a woman and a man knows how a woman makes him feel, then he may not be able to compete for her love juices and a woman knows what a woman knows. And it is his entire fault for leaving her in need for sexual activities with him, her husband, the one who she is supposed to be with. I don't feel sorry for him, and if he should lose her, then he will just have to live with the whole damn bit. How in the world will I tell Tyrone something like this about his best friend's wife? One thing for sure and that is, I will no longer be having difficulties getting with him during our midday getaway when he hears about this. Tyrone will not gamble on me finding something better, and especially with a woman." Monique continued into deep thoughts on her and Tyrone.

"Well, I am pulling into my driveway and thank goodness Tyrone is not home yet. This gives me a chance to prepare dinner early and get the kids off to bed early. Tyrone and I need to be alone when we talk, and I know he will be using a lot of (not for our children's ears) kind of words. It's a good thing I picked up the kids before coming home first because it's going to give me more time to have everything in place for an early dinner.

"It's after six o'clock and Tyrone has not come home yet. I hope the reason he is running late today is because he is talking to Lacy. As a matter of fact, it better be the only reason outside of an emergency situation. It's a good thing I still got some trust in that man; and I got a whole lot of love to go with it. Tyrone knows what side of his bread is buttered, oops speaking to self again. And speaking of the former devil, he's home!"

"Tyrone sweetheart, I have been waiting to give you some good news and some not so good news, but it is not all bad. Did you get a chance to talk to Lacy today?" "Monique, things are worse than I thought. That jackass thinks that he is in love with Samantha. He said that he has been thinking about a separation and eventually, a divorce from Imani. I had no idea things was that bad with him and Imani. I wish there were something we could do, but when I think about it, the more I think we better stay out of it. I thought he was my best friend, but I guess he didn't trust me enough to confide in me."

"Tyrone, I was going to wait until after dinner, but I can't hold this from you any longer. I want you to sit with both feet down on the floor. Don't say a word because baby, I got something to tell you that will knock those socks off your feet. I had a long talk with Imani today and she told me that she was having an affair. I thought that would get your attention. What I am going to say next is going to blow your mind. Shhhh, no talking for the next few minutes. You remember my girlfriend who we call Brown Sugar and sometimes Ms. B don't you?" "I remember that loud underclass group of women you and Imani used to hang out with sometimes, and one of them was called Ms. B, but what about these people, and how do they play a part in what our friends are going through?" Mrs. Imani Ball and Ms. B are lovers. (Pause) You can close your mouth now, Tyrone." "Monique, what will Lacy do when he hears about this?" "What he is going to hear about my dear husband is, that his manhood got knocked out of the box by a woman, and I love it, I just love it, so let the dog think about that one while he is screwing Ms. Samantha, and Ms. B is laying the same kind of good loving on Imani that Samantha is laying on him, I love it, I love it, I love it, I just love it, and what is he going to do about it, not a damn thing."

"Well, lover boy, I still plan to send the kids off to bed early so that we may have a little more time together. And I do plan to rock your world tonight in a way it has never been rocked before. I have practiced in my mind on some things that I will be experimenting on you, so plan to rise to a powerful plain of ecstasy where you have never been with me before. The action will start promptly at nine o'clock p.m. in the master bedroom."

"Tyrone, how are you feeling this morning?" "Baby, the only thought I have on my mind at this moment is, last night, "I touched a dream." "Ha, ha, ha, ha, Tyrone, why don't you stay in bed this morning and let me bring our breakfast to the bedroom. I was thinking that since we have a long evening ahead of us, maybe we should stay in bed a little longer this morning. Guests for our dinner cocktail party will be arriving between 6p.m. and 7p.m. this evening and I want to be well rested when they arrive. I will be back with our breakfast as soon as I give Angel and Ty, Jr. their breakfast."

"Monique, thank you for making me so comfortable and making me feel so great at a time when I really needed it. Baby, no matter what anyone else sees in you, in my eyes, you're perfect to me. After I have finished eating breakfast, I think I will lie here and watch a little television for a couple of hours and maybe take a nap." "I will not disturb you, sweetheart, I will be checking throughout the house to make sure everything is in place for tonight. I will check with the caterers and make sure they are here on time. I will let you take care of the beverages. I don't know about you but I feel like listening to old school jazz tonight. I can just hear my man Hank Crawford doing his thing on his sax, playing, "Help Me Make It Through The Night."

"I sure hope Imani comes tonight even if Lacy doesn't. No matter what happens between her and Lacy, she will always be my best friend. We will still hang together and she will still be invited to social events at my home. I don't think Lacy would dare bring another woman to my home, knowing that Imani is my best friend. He has a warped sense of humor if he thinks that I can or will be friendly with his other woman. Sweetheart, if you hear sounds coming from my mouth, don't worry about it, I'm just talking to myself. And I ain't crazy, I heard you in there. I am just across the way in my dressing room."

"Messing around with my old high school buddies is enough to make me crazy. And whatever Imani sees in another woman is a puzzle to me, and of all people, Brown Sugar. But I suppose it's just me who can't seem to get with it. Somehow, I just can't get past the male gender to even foster the thought of being with another woman. Damn, she's got the same thing I got, and I want something different when I'm in bed to get it on with my partner, not the same damn kind of stuff I carry around with me all the time. If it's what Imani wants, then I'll support her all the way. But my husband will never know. Wow, am I in deep thought!"

As Monique continues in deep thought, "with all these clothes in this closet, I know I should be able to find something that will stop them in their tracks. I think I will get devilish tonight and ware this daring black dress. I love showing off my designer clothes because people will be able to see the line of clothing I have at my boutique. Tyrone has a white suit and black vest that looks very manly on him and I think that I will ask him to wear it tonight. We will be the gorgeous couple we always are when we are socializing with our friends and Tyrone's business associates from his law office."

"Tyrone, don't forget to check with your friend at the jazz club to make sure he knows what time you want him to be here to start serving drinks to our guests. The liquor was delivered earlier while you were taking a nap. You can relax, I have checked everything, and this evening's event is well set. All we need is our guests for the completion. Don't get up just yet, sweetheart. I think I will join you in bed. I need to relax my body and my mind for a little while before taking a shower and getting dressed for the party."

TOTAL RELAXATION REJUVENATES THE BODY

....

Two hours later

"Tyrone, I think it is time for both of us to get up." "Thanks, baby for your way of helping me to relax. I think I put you in a temporary coma also. Monique, we are so good for each other, and that is why God put us together. I am no longer feeling stressed, as a matter of fact, I feel good, and I can see you're glowing as always after we have completed our oneness."

"Lying here quietly, it is amazing how I always manage to flash back to some of the conversations Tyrone and I had early in our marriage. He said in one of our conversations shortly after our honeymoon, that once he enters my body and I receive him in a spiritual connection, it takes our minds to the same wave links merged as one, which connects our souls as one. I suppose such as it is meant to be in a marriage when it is done in the name of the Father, the Son and the Holy Spirit. The man talks to me in a way where I always feel good about honoring him. He always shows much love in his conversations with me. I am so proud to be his wife. I know that I am living on top of the rainbow right now, and I am going to make it last for as long as possible. And I pray that it is forever which translates into until death shall we part. Here I am again mumbling about my good thoughts about Tyrone. Lordy, lordy, lordy help the man if he messes up, and it is not meant as a prayer."

Seven

6:30 p.m. guests arriving for the party

……………………………………………

"Good evening, Mr. and Mrs. Smith, do come in, it is so good to see you, as you can see some of our guests have already arrived. Please join us and remember that whatever kind of drinks you desire, our bartender Sam, who is fantastic with his mixes, can whip it up for you. Tyrone, sweetheart, will you please stay near the door for a little while to greet our guests, I need to speak with the caterer. I need to make sure everything is set up in the kitchen properly for fast service and fast cleanup if needed."

Monique goes to the kitchen and stays just long enough to make sure that everything is running smoothly, she then hurries back to the party where Tyrone is at the door greeting guests. Both Monique and Tyrone are all smiles because they know that this is a successful evening for them. The music is great and the drinks are great, and so will the food, which is on top of the list for making of a good party.

"Sweetheart, everything is running smoothly in the kitchen, how are things going out here among the partying people?" "It's jumping out here, the music is great, the drinks are great, and once the food comes out, then everything will be great." Monique looks startled, "Oh, my gosh! Tyrone why didn't you tell me that Lacy was here? He better not have brought another woman with him. Talk to me, Tyrone, Why is Lacy here without Imani?" "I'm sorry, baby; I tried to prolong it for as long as possible before telling you that Lacy is here with Samantha. Baby, you must keep in mind that Samantha is your client in a way because of her line of designer clothing that will be coming to your store. Monique, please, help me keep this party running smoothly. I don't want other people's drama played out in our home tonight."

ALL HELL IS ABOUT TO BREAK LOOSE

……………………………………………………...

"Sweetheart will you please get the door; I think I need to get myself a drink right now. Sam, will you mix the strongest drink that you think I can handle without collapsing into a drunken coma which will be a disaster. I believe all hell will break loose soon and I want to be drunk enough for it. Sam, you know Lacy's wife, Imani don't you? Well, she may come here tonight because she is my best friend and she is invited to the party this evening and as you can see, Lacy is here with another woman." "Oh shit----please forgive me, Ms. Monique, for using that word in your home and in your presence, I am so sorry but it slipped out when I saw Mrs. Ball walk in through that door." Monique whirled and did a double take when Sam said that. "Í must find Tyrone and fine him fast."

Monique couldn't believe her eyes, just as she was about to walk over to greet Imani, in through the door walks in Ms. B, Detroit's one and only Brown Sugar, Ms. Popular. Now this is about the time something usually hits the fan, but all is well so far. Lacy and Imani have seen each other, but neither one knows about the other's date. Monique is thinking "tonight is one that nobody will ever believe. Hell, I'm here and I don't believe it."

"Tyrone, Imani is here and I don't want her to see Lacy with another woman." Well, Mrs. Monique, my dear baby, and I don't want him to see her with another woman. I am getting a bit anxious about all this freaking mess and I am about ready to sit back and watch an episode of, "Two Hens and a Rooster", with the first episode coming to you from the Haywill mansion located on top of the hill in living color."

SOMETHING HAS JUST HIT THE FAN

…………………………………………….

Imani looks across the room and sees Lacy's arms around Samantha. Almost instantaneously, Lacy looks up from his attention on Samantha and he is looking Imani in her face. In that same moment the sound of the saxophone in the jazz piece by Hank Crawford "Help Me Make It Through The Night" engulfed the entire room, if not the whole house. He walked quickly toward Imani as if to cut her off before she could come over to where he was with Samantha. Just as Lacy got close to Imani something happened. Imani turned facing Brown Sugar and gave her a big loving kiss on her mouth, she then turned to Lacy with her arms around Brown sugar and with a sensuous smile, she said to him, "I hope you are enjoying yourself this evening, my dear husband, I certainly am enjoying myself." The whole room was frozen and everybody was speechless.

"Tyrone, I don't think we have enough liquor in the house to smother this one. Can you believe what just happened and what in the world was she thinking about and better yet, what in the hell has she been smoking? Tyrone, don't just look at me like that, and anyway, you know you can't find a damn thing in a bottle to make a person become that bold and crazy. The person would have to be already crazy to pull a stunt like that, especially at my well planned sophisticated party. Tyrone just don't talk to me right now, I can see you are acting crazy too. Wrong is wrong I don't care if she is my best friend. If you give me that look again I am going to smack you and I don't care who sees it."

Monique turned and ran upstairs as fast as her high heels could carry her. "Monique wait for me, slow down, we do need to talk and we need to do it right away. Tyrone caught up with Monique in the Master Bedroom and began talking to her. "What Imani did really surprised me, but whatever that Brown Sugar does is what I expect of her. I've told you more than once, and I don't mind repeating it, the woman has no class. You can take the pig out of the pen but she is still a mess. Imani needs to get from under her clutches. I don't know how you can stand to spend any of your time in that person's life. Just don't let her turn you against man---- as if that could ever happen. You know you love this man's tool too much to make a trade." "You got that right; now give me one of your lingering kisses."

"Oh no, not now, baby why did you do that to me when you know we got guests downstairs!" Too late, now we have to take care of each other, and be quiet about it. I don't know about you but I want my dessert and I want it now."

Twenty Minutes Later

....

"The last one downstairs will have to cater to the other for the rest of the night." The two quickly made themselves presentable and raced down stairs. "Baby, you took too much wind out of me when we were upstairs, that was the only way you were able to beat me downstairs." "I am so glad I won, and now Lacy will see how a husband is supposed to treat his wife."

"Sweetheart, will you please get me a drink, you know what I like." "Whatever my little sweet potato wants she gets. Will that be all for my baby? Monique, I know you are up to something, but whatever it is, don't you let it blow up in this house this evening, please. I am going to talk to Lacy tonight and find out what is going on with him. He surprised me tonight by bringing another woman and not his wife to my home and that is not like him to disrespect another man's home, especially his best friend's home." Later at the party the two men were able to talk.

"Lacy, man, we got to talk. What made you bring Samantha here tonight, after all, you do know Imani is Monique's best friend and she would most likely come to the party with or without you." "Tyrone, I don't know what is happening with me. Somehow Samantha has me doing things I know I should not be doing. It is so crazy for me now. I can't seem to get it together. I still have love for Imani, after all we have two beautiful daughters together, and I know this sounds crazy but I am in love with Samantha also."

"Tyrone, you are my best friend, I need help in a bad way, tell me something." "Lacy my man, your wife is my wife's best friend and I can't get caught up in this one. I'm sorry, Lacy but you can't count on your best friend with this, I have my wife to think about and I know you wouldn't want my home life to be in a bad way because I got caught up in your love triangle would you? I know if I did, without a doubt, I would have hell to pay. And I definitely wouldn't want to go there." "I understand my friend, and I am sorry for showing disrespect to your home by bringing Samantha here tonight."

"I remember when tonight would have been a great time for us with our wives together. I feel hurt and with embarrassment about Imani and another woman, and somehow I still can't believe what I saw. I cannot allow her to do this with our daughters living in our home. I don't want them exposed to such a thing." "Lacy, what in the hell are you talking about, don't you know it will hurt your girls if they find out that you are leaving their mother for another woman. I don't see what she is doing is so much different from what you are doing. You both are wrong and you are out of your cotton-picking-mind if you think you can pack your belongings and move out and not cause trauma to your daughters. You and Imani need to get back together and work on your marriage for the sake of your children. If Imani was doing half the things Monique is doing to keep me on my toes, the two of you would be together tonight. That woman got me coming home when I know I'm supposed to be someplace else. Now that's a hell of a woman. Work on what you got before you trade it in. Give her good reasons for wanting to take care of her man. This is my advice to my best friend."

"Well, sweetheart, I must say last night was a night to remember. I know our guests have something to gossip about today. Since I am not going to church this morning, why don't we just lounge around our bedroom and talk, play, make love or whatever." "Baby, what about all three and no whatever." "Sounds good to me but first we must talk about those screwed up people we call our best friends." "No, first take care of your husband; he needs care now, big-time. You know you have been my caffeine for years. So work it girl, surprise me this morning before I lay mine on you." "Man just let me first look in on the kids. I'm sure they're still asleep because they never go to sleep early when we have these parties. If they are still asleep we can get down with our business and afterward we can all have breakfast together, how does that sound?" "You're the boss of this household." "And don't forget it, Mr. Head of this household."

Two hours later at the Haywill breakfast table, "No coffee for me Monique, I'll have just orange juice. I will also have whatever you're preparing for Angel and Ty, Jr. I feel like eating this morning, since I don't usually get Sunday morning breakfast, with you hurrying off to church every Sunday."

"And the head of this household should be right there with me. Don't get me started this morning Tyrone, especially on Sunday morning."

"Baby, why don't we lounge on the patio near the pool and just talk to each other while enjoying this nice weather in these calm surroundings we are blessed with. I will take you and the kids out for an early dinner. I would also like to do something with you that we have not done since our courting days and that is for the two of us to stay up all night talking. I know you remember those beautiful courtship days when we were trying to learn about each other. We would hold hands and look into each other's eyes longing to be kissed by the other. Our love was strong then and fifteen years later it is even stronger. Let us go back to when we first got together and you were working hard at getting your boutique set up and Lacy and I had just started our career opening a law firm together. I had a small place back then and I must say that tiny apartment got a lot of action back then. I would be high on just the chemistry of your body."

"Tyrone, if walls could talk we would have been arrested for indecent exposure. And back then, we were young and ready to try anything goofy or awkward or just plain crazy to do. Remember when we use to do it two, three, four and sometimes five different ways and we would later have long discussions about which position was most satisfying measuring our pleasure on a scale one to five. We would choose two or three of the possible best. We would then try the chosen ones and narrow it down to the very best we both agreed was it." "Tyrone, that was so much fun but we were young when we were doing those things. We were so good with each other." "Monique, I love you so much and baby, thank you for fifteen beautiful years. I am looking for many more beautiful blessed years with you." "Thank you Tyrone, now why don't you put on some old school jams. I feel like hearing that great sound by the O'Jays "Forever Mine."

"Tyrone, I can't help but think about what is happening with Imani and Lacy. They were married two years after we were married and now they are talking about ending their marriage. I am sad just thinking about it. Sweetheart, why don't you make reservations on Mackinac Island for the four of us for next weekend?" "Now Monique, whatever plan you got working in your mind, forget it. Those two people will have to come together on their own and if they cannot, then maybe they should get a divorce." "Not if I can help it, Mr. Haywill. Never, let it be known that I Monique Haywill turned her back on her best friend." "Monique, I believe that interference in other people lives can do nothing but cause more trauma to the already bad situation. When someone come to you and ask you for help in a situation, then you have been given permission to interfere. Until that happens you need to butt out." "Tyrone but...."Tyrone but nothing, Just cool it Monique, Imani and Lacy are our best friends, not our children,, and like I said, you need to butt out. I mean it Monique, being a best friend doesn't give you the right to interfere in that friend's life. I love you Monique, and you need to listen to me sometimes. Why don't we give them a chance to work out their problems on their own and we will be here for them if they need us." "I agree with you Tyrone, and thanks."

Eight

MEANTIME AT THE BEAUTY SHOP

....

Ms. B could hardly wait to get to her beauty shop the next morning to tell the girls and Luscious about what happened at Monique's house the night before. There she was acting out the whole scene and giving everybody a good belly laugh. "Ladies, you should have seen Lacy Ball's face when Imani gave me a big kiss on my mouth; she did it in front of everybody there at the party. Imani and I are no longer a secret because the secret is out now. I am expecting that Ms. high-class Monique to come into my shop today. I know she is Imani's best friend but she better not come in here starting nothing because if she does then I got something for her sophisticated ass. Imani is with me and there isn't a damn thing she can do about it. Ladies, Imani is in the back room resting. I will go back there to talk with her later. I think maybe she needs another hour to relax. While I'm back there just call me if you need me for anything or if Monique comes in. Please don't send her to the back."

Almost two hours later, Monique burst through the door of Ms. B's Beauty Shop as if she was trying to catch her man with another woman. "Where is Brown Sugar? I want to see her right now. Is she in the back room? I'm going back there and if any one of you ladies and you too, Luscious, just try me, you better plan for a piece of my ass because if you try me, I'll be coming after yours." "Please, Ms. Monique, we don't want any trouble, I will get Ms. B for you." Luscious hurried off to let Ms. B know that Monique was out in the shop and is threatening to come to the back to look for Ms. Imani. "I can hear that big mouth of hers straight to the back of this shop. I'm on my way out there to talk to her right now. The nerve of that woman coming here to my place of business talking loud and making demands. Imani is a grown woman with a mind of her own and she can do whatever she is pleased to do and with whomever she is pleased to do it with and without permission from nobody."

As Brown Sugar, who is also called Ms. B, reaches the front of the shop Monique is still at it in full blast, "tell her to bring her ass up front or I will come back there" and she let everybody know what to expect if she has to go back there. Monique turned and she was almost nose to nose with Brown sugar. "What is all that noise out here? Monique, what in the hell are you doing in my shop, disturbing my staff, and so early in the morning too. Unless you are getting service, I'm going to have to ask you to leave. This is a place of business and I will not have you upsetting the ladies in my beauty shop." "I am not leaving until I find out where Imani is. I called her home this morning and the babysitter said that she came home late last night and left early this morning. The babysitter said that she had not planned to be there today to care for her twin girls but now it looks like she will have to stay over until either Imani or Lacy comes home, and she said she hasn't seen Mr. Ball at all. If Imani is with you, I just want to talk to her. As a matter of fact, I don't plan to leave here until I have talked with her. Now you will either bring her out here to see me or I will go to the back room to see her, you take your pick, Ms. BS, and if you want trouble, I will give you trouble. Go ahead and call the police, I don't care, and by the time they get here there will be a reason for me to go to jail. Now which will it be, Imani coming out here or me going back there?"

Imani finally comes from the back, on her own. “Monique, you are so loud. I was in the back trying to get some sleep, what is the matter with you, acting like this.” “Imani, if you’re so sleepy why don’t you go home and sleep in a comfortable bed instead of on a cot in the back room of this low class dump of a so called beauty shop. Why don’t we go back to your place and after you have rested the two of us can sit down and talk. I want you to feel free to talk to me about anything you want to talk about, and to you, Ms. B, You need to get some church in you because you need Jesus in you and in your life.” “Ms. Know-it-all, I got my condo, my big screen TV and Pastor Joel O’Steen, Potter’s House with Bishop T.D. Jakes, Pastor Creflo Dollar, and other messengers from God coming into my crib all the time, and further more, I do have a church home, which means you do not know me, Ms. Bourgeois heifer, don’t be so quick to judge me. I know that you’re in the church but, is the church in you? That is the question, Ms. Stuck up lady. If I fall to the wayside, the Bible, which is the “WORD”, commissioned you as a Christian woman to pick me up, straighten me out and turn me around. Now put that in your horn and blow.

BACK AT THE BALL'S MANSION

....

"Monique that nap was the best thing that I needed at this time. I feel so much better than I felt this morning. I feel like my life is so messed up right now, what am I to do, my marriage is falling apart and I go and do something to make it worse. Thank you, Monique, for being here for me. I am so much in love with my husband, and I want him back." "And you will get him back. We just have to work on it, and on that Samantha, the husband snatcher."

"Imani, once we put our heads together that Lacy will not know what hit him. We will go after him ghetto style, hard but mellow. Imani, you may have been born and raised middle class but you need to learn how to go ghetto style with your love making on Lacy. Give him something different once in a while. Tyrone and I like to get down naughty nasty at least once a month, and believe me, once a month is all he can take. When we go at it hard and strong everything goes, nothing held back, a little bit of this and a little bit of that, sometimes starting on the bed and ending on the floor. I think since we've been married we have performed every way possible, some positions I couldn't do now if I wanted to. What I am trying to say is, for me that could be only for me and my husband. I am a one man's woman. I can't think of a reason why I would want to be with another man and, in your case, another woman and give away the most precious inner part of me, my soul, which is my all."

"I know you have a lot of work to do on your marriage and I will be available for you as a friend 24/7. I will be with you until the end, whether it's good or bad. Imani, I want you to seriously pray and ask God for help. Even after you come out of this, you are going to need help. You can count on me to be here for you, and you can talk while I do nothing but listen. I am going home now so that I can be there when Tyrone comes home. I will keep in touch with you, and please keep in mind that some of the things we talked about are for the ears of us two only. Try to get plenty rest so that you will look good every time Lacy lays eyes on you. Bye now." "Bye Monique, and again, thanks for being here for me in my time of need. Best friends forever?" "Best friends forever."

Monique is in deep thought again, "I must find a way to get through to Tyrone so that he will at least try to encourage Lacy to give his marriage a chance by going to marriage counseling, and also to remind his friend that he is still a married man, and that he owes his wife, the mother of his children, her due respect as a wife, if nothing else. I sure hope Tyrone made reservations for the four of us to go to Mackinac Island next weekend. That would mean he got Lacy to agree to go there to be with Imani, if nothing else but to talk. The reason I didn't say anything to Imani is because I didn't want to get her hopes up and then there is a letdown. She does not need added on hurt when it comes to her husband."

PUTTING FRIENDSHIP BEFORE MONEY
(After a brief meeting with Samantha Skye)

....

"I am so sorry Ms. Skye, but I must cancel our contract for your line of designer clothes in my store. Before you try to fight the contract, I advise you to read the fine print at the bottom of the contract. It is written that, "if anytime there is a discrepancy in the working relationship that would affect the business due to indifferences between the owner and the person who he/she is in contract with, the owner has the right to break the contract between the two said parties. As I think you already know, Mrs. Imani Ball, Lacy's wife is my best friend and she also acts as my advisor for my business when I need someone's input that only a female can give concerning women's clothing styles that compliment with comfort and can be worn with all other styles. So, Ms. Samantha, as you like to be called, I don't need your kind of trouble in my life or my business. My family and my friends are important to me, so here is a letter explaining everything. Also, attached to the letter is a notarized copy of the dismissal of the contract between the two of us. You may try to fight this contract in the court of law and you will lose. I don't think Lacy is going to pay out big bucks to an attorney who will most likely be my husband or another friend in the mix, to represent the other woman who he is committing adultery with. What you need to do is crawl back under that slimy demonic rock from which you came and leave good folks alone."

After Monique finished speaking her piece, she quickly moved from her chair and walked across the room to the door and opened it for Samantha to make her exit from the building. Samantha hurriedly walked out the door and suddenly stopped with a pause. She then did an about-face, but before she could say a word, Monique slammed the door shut. "Damn you" was all Samantha could say before turning and with a huff she made a dash toward her car.

On the other side of the door Monique could hear rubber squeaking as Samantha sped away. She did a dance while laughing about her accomplishment in dealing with Samantha the witch bitch. She held her head back and screamed the words out "HOT DAG-IT, A GOOD DAY AFTER ALL."

Nine

Samantha is very angry about the letter she has received from Monique. As a matter of fact she is angry to the point of talking to herself. "If she thinks that she can treat me any kind of way she wants to and get away with it, she had better think again because Samantha Skye is not the one she wants to tangle with. That miss goody two-shoe, Monique, is in for revenge that will come at her like lightning after thunder. When I finish with her she will regret the day she pissed me off. Lacy will not push me to the side for nobody, not even his wife. What Samantha wants, Samantha gets and what

Samantha decides to keep, nobody will take it away. The city of Detroit will know that, this city molded little country girl has arrived, and nobody, I repeat, nobody and I mean nobody will mess over me and not feel the power of my backlash. I must be really mad to be standing here talking to myself."

A WEEKEND ON MACKINAC ISLAND

....

"Monique, I don't know how I'm going to ever pay Tyrone back for making this weekend possible for me to try and work things out with Lacy. How in the world did Tyrone get Lacy to share a hotel room with me? Monique, I think my prayers are being answered." Tyrone spoke quickly, "Ladies, we are going to take our bags to our rooms and in about thirty minutes we will go to the dining room for lunch. Is that alright with everybody? Lacy, Monique and I will meet you and Imani downstairs in the lounging area before we go to lunch, wait for us there." Both couples separated and went to their rooms to unpack and freshen up for lunch.

"Tyrone, the room is very nice, and stop looking at that bed; I can read your mind very clearly." "Baby, you know what this reminds me of and I can see the look in your eyes too." "Yes, but we need to take our minds off ourselves for a little while. This weekend is very important for Imani and Lacy and we need to talk and come up with ways for them to put some love back in their marriage. I don't think they should dwell on their outside affairs until they have rekindled a little romance and put remembrance of their sex life back in play and back in bed. I want them to enjoy this weekend together."

"Tyrone, sweetheart, we will have our time together, but we both must remember the reason we're here. We must not lose focus on the reason we're here. Now give me a kiss and hold me in your arms for a moment." "Baby, you have always been so good to me and for me. What would you do if you ever found out that I was having an affair with another woman or just the opposite, such as with your friend, Imani?" Tyrone, don't you dare even think it because I refuse to go into that kind of competition, and as for a woman, that is an automatic beat down, and you don't even want to know what is in store for you. You don't have to worry because you wouldn't know what the hell hit you anyway." "Woman, you are scaring me with a threat like that." "Sweetheart, it is not a threat, it is just fact for you." "Now you are really scaring me."

Monique is in deep thought again as she ponders on the conversation she just had with her husband. "I don't know why a man thinks that he can do anything he wants to do and get away with it. I love my husband, but if he makes an enemy out of me, then I will have to go at him like an enemy. Just think about it, I know that I will do everything that I can possibly do to keep my marriage together, but to give to someone else what I think should be solely mine would be like cutting my heart out piece by piece, hurt by hurt, leaving me slowly dying inside. Just thinking about it makes me want to find out where Tyrone is when I can't reach him, and I know he is not in court some of those times. Whatever is happening on the dark side will certainly surface slowly but surely with the whole nasty truth in daylight. If something should come to light, he had better fly high in an eagle's ass and pray that the bitch don't shit. Enough of these crazy thoughts that are running through my mind, my imagination is running wild and crazy with me."

A CHAMPAGNE ATMOSPHERE LUNCH

....

"Tyrone, you are so romantic, it is just like you to choose the garden setting for us to have lunch. The champagne looks cold and inviting, doesn't it, Imani?" "Yes it does, and the setting is made for a couple on their honeymoon. Lacy, thanks, for having me here this weekend." "No problem, enjoy." "Sweetheart, why don't you and Lacy go ahead and order our lunch while Imani and I go to the lady's room." "Monique, what are you up to? I just left my room a few minutes ago and I have no need to see a lady's room, anyway, I just left the mirror in my hotel room and my makeup is still fresh, including my lipstick. what's going on in that scheming little head of yours, girlfriend? I hope it's something that will make this weekend work for me, if you know what I mean."

After about five minutes, Monique and Imani are back at the table with their husbands. "Well, ladies, I hope you like what we picked from the menu for you. Imani and Lacy, I would like to make a toast to you, but first I want to thank my beautiful wife, Monique, for coming up with the idea of a weekend on Mackinac Island for the four of us." "Let me make the toast, sweetheart, after all you said it was my idea for our best friends to be here with us. I toast to you, Mr. and Mrs. Ball, my words of encouragement. May this weekend bring a renewal of the oneness of two souls already joined in the spirit by God in Holy matrimony, and may you recapture all the good things that are slipping away, because they are worth saving. Tyrone, it's your turn to say something". "Baby, you have said it all, let's just eat." "What did I do or say that was wrong?" "Nothing, you're just as always, perfect, now let's eat damn-it."

"We hate to eat and run but Imani and I are going to take a nice long nap before dinner." "Why don't you call our room or my cell phone or Monique's cell phone around dinner time and maybe we all can ride the horse and buggy to a restaurant away from the hotel for dinner." "Sounds great to me, and from the smile on Imani's face, she agrees, so we will be joining you at dinner time."

COULD THERE BE TROUBLE IN PARADISE

....

"Tyrone, I know this hotel room has two beds but we have never slept in separate beds all the years we've been married, so why are you making yourself comfortable in the other bed? Whatever it was that I said or done, I didn't do it on purpose, and sweetheart I am truly sorry if I did something to upset you, please forgive me." "I forgive you, but baby it always seems as if you are trying to upstage me when we're with friends." "Tyrone, I never realized I was doing that. I know my place as your wife and I also know that when you shine, your wife shines. Come over to my bed and let's get closer while we talk." A little while later lying in bed relaxed, "baby it's almost dinnertime, you sure know how to relax your husband, and it's all good."

Back in Detroit, Rrrring, Rrrring, Rrrring, "hello, this is the Ball's resident, how may I help you?" "You may help me by either putting the man of the house, Mr., Ball, on the phone or by telling me how I may be able to reach him because he is not answering his cell phone. Who are you anyway, answering his home phone?" "I am the baby sitter and you can reach Mr., Ball by calling his wife's cell phone." "Will you please tell me where he is." "No." Click went the sound of the phone, and then silence.

"If that Lacy Ball thinks that he can push me off so easy, he better think about it again. He can't screw me and later it's going to be, to hell with Samantha. Oh no, I don't roll that way. I will no longer be the other woman or his closet freak. Lacy is in my life now and not even that busy body Monique Haywill can do anything about it. My question is, why is he with that damn wife of his, I thought I had broken that up for good. I can see now that I have a lot of work cut out for me. I have never been and never will be a wham-bam-thank-you-ma'me whore and I don't do booty calls. Lacy is my man and my plan is to keep it that way because I have fallen in love with that man. I will not give him up, not even for his wife."

IN LACY'S AND IMANI'S HOTEL ROOM ON THE ISLAND
(12:00 midnight)

....

Imani steps out from the bathroom and stood half way between the bathroom door and the bed where Lacy was stretched out watching a movie on the cable channel. He had a surprised look on his face as he lifted his head from the pillar. "Damn, you look good standing there in the raw with your hair flowing. Come here woman, now. Yes master, Imani responded in her playful way. They both laughed as she lay beside him." "Do you remember that weekend we went with Tyrone and Monique to their favorite hotel, the Embassy Suites in Livonia, or was it Southfield? Anyway, they had no idea that at that time we had not yet shared our love juices. I was so much afraid I wouldn't be able to satisfy you in the way of total completion." "Ohoooooo, do I ever remember that first night, I have never been turned on and turned out so complete." "Oh, I also remember that first time. I too, had never been turned on and turned out so complete. When we finished I was totally satisfied and exhausted to the point where I didn't have the energy to roll over and out of the puddle of wetness I was laying in. Lacy, we were so good for each other over the years, what happened to us to make us act the way we do? I want to know so that I can start working on making our marriage good again, and I am not saying this for the sake of the twins, it is for me. I need you Lacy, and I know now that I am no good without you in my life as my husband, I want you to be more to me than just my baby's daddy." "Baby, we are going to talk, but right now, I just want to lay here peacefully with you in my arms and quietly thank God for giving us this chance to know each other again."

SOUL LOVE

The soul of love is housed within
It's filtered through the heart by-way to first begin
Taking in strong exciting feelings with unending joy
Accepting love's pure warm honey as in girl and boy
The words "I love you" doesn't always mean "I do"
But action with investment says "I'm in love with you"
The key to keeping love alive is to let it surface everyday
And let it be with fun to share each and everyway
Accept no negative advice that your choice is not good
Through faith and God's promise It's clearly understood
Whom God put together let no one stand in their way
To under-mind blessed love you'll surely have to pay
It's not always easy to know if true love is truly true
Just listen to your heart for what you're moved do
If you believe in blessings bestowed from above
You, a true believer, have found **SOUL LOVE.**

BACK IN DETROIT
(A visit to the hood)

....

As Samantha rides around in an area where she was told that she would find Brown Sugar's Beauty Shop, she was in deep thoughts. "I can't believe that I, Samantha Skye, am actually lowering my standards for the sake of a man. I guess revenge comes in all categories, and this one is going to be a mother. Lacy will feel the scorn of this woman. My biggest problem now is how the hell I am going to get the queen of the ghetto to help me with my plan. I am banking on the idea of her getting revenge on Imani for getting back with her husband, Lacy."

As Samantha enters Brown Sugar Beauty Shop she is well noticed. "Well, I be damned, Avenue of Fashion in the house. Girls, look who just walked into Brown Sugar's place! What a surprise so early in the morning, how can I help you, Ms. High-almighty?" "Ms. B, I would like to speak with you in private please." "Ms. Fashion Thing, this is as private as you're gonna get in this place, now what's up?" "As you know, I am a friend of Lacy Ball." "No Ms. Thing, you're Lacy's bitch in the streets. Now what is it you're trying to tell me?" "Ms. B, I need you to help me with getting Lacy away from his wife. As of this moment they are together and the babysitter refused to tell me where they are. I have not seen Lacy in two days, and that is too long for him and his wife to be together without interruption from me as a reminder of the other side of love, if you know what I mean." "I know exactly what you mean, and girl you are just what I heard about you, no good. What is it you want me to do that you can't do yourself? Imani and I are not just lovers, and we have been friends since high school. As a matter of fact, along with Monique, we were a threesome back in the day. The only reason I lean so hard on Monique is because she needs to get off that high horse she's riding sometimes." "Never mind, you couldn't help me anyway. I'll do whatever I need to do to get the job done." "Get what job done? Ms Thing, I know you didn't come here to try and get me to do harm to my friend. You better get the hell out my shop before I do harm to your ass. And stay out." **Slam----**sound of the door.

"I will deal with that Ms. B at a later date, but right now I have a bigger fish to fry. Lacy has more to lose than me. He has both, a wife and children, and I also know that he loves those children dearly. If anything should happen to those twins of his he would be destroyed. If he kicks me to the side like an old shoe, I will destroy him and It will be all his fault for romancing me and making me fall in love with him. Before I walk away from it all, he will see me as a woman he wish that he never met and could forget she ever existed. He will for the rest of his life think of me as poison, the most deadly one. One day when he least expects it, I will step right into his space and destroy him in a way that would make Hell look like a not-not-so-bad place to be.

IS A SECOND HONEYMOON IN THE WORKS?

……………………………………………………...

"Lacy, it's almost dinner time, and we have not talked yet. There is so much I want to say to you and there is so much I want to hear from you." "Imani honey, after that performance you just gave me, all I can say is,
Number one……I love you
Number two……I love you
Number three…..I love you
And our third finger left hand, wear our commitment to each other. Baby I am still in love with you and thank you for the reminder. I needed this kind of jolt to wake me up. Let's just lie here in each other's arms for a little while before we shower and dress for dinner but first we need to call Monique and Tyrone to let them know that we might be a little late." "Honey, I'll take care of that right now."

Rrrrring, Rrrrring, Rrrrring "Hello, oh, hi Imani, I was not expecting you to call so early, are you and Lacy ready to go out for dinner already?" "No, I was calling to tell you that Lacy and I will not be ready for about an hour later than we had planned. Is that all right with you and Tyrone?" "Yes, take all the time you need, Tyrone and I are in no rush to go out anyway." After hanging the phone up Monique smiled and said to Tyrone, "I am so happy Imani and Lacy need more time because it could mean that they are busy doing something good. "Monique, I am going downstairs to the restaurant to get coffee and something for us to snack on. I know how coffee perks you up. I am glad you told Imani and Lacy to take all the time they need. The more they talk and be together, the better the chance is for them to get a strong hold on what they are trying to master in their relationship, and with that they can go home renewed in their "oneness" as you always say, and that is something the other woman can never master." "You got that right, sweetheart, now give your baby a kiss before you take your fine self out that door. (Slam)------- I do love that man."

Being on an Island with no cars and just horses and buggies seems to make everything move at a slower pace. It is such a relaxed feeling and the picture view shows nothing but continued flows of flower gardens. The only thing you may turn your nose up at is, as you cross the narrow streets you must be careful because the horses are constantly walking and dropping horse waste along the streets. It is a wonderful place to go for a honeymoon and beautiful sights to view while walking and holding hands. "Well, Lacy my man, I can truthfully say that our wives are the two most beautiful women on the Island. Can we pick'em, or can we pick'em."
"Why don't you gloating husbands pick a restaurant and feed us." "Now Monique, you know there is no picking of restaurants in a place this small. We will stop at the first place we see that might be available for our accommodation and enjoy this special time as we also enjoy the great food." "Tyrone, let's not forget to buy souvenirs to take back home and also a special keepsake as a reminder of this very special

trip. Now let's get to stepping so that I can eat, I'm hungry."

Ten

(7:00 Saturday morning)

....

"Lacy darling, we have done it again. We did everything but talk about our problems. We should not go back to Detroit before resolving some of our issues. This is our last day here before leaving early tomorrow morning for home." "Imani, you are right and I will start by going downstairs to the restaurant and getting us breakfast and of course your caffeine coffee, ha ha. We will not leave this room until dinnertime, and if need, we will not leave until tomorrow morning to go back to the Metro. You're my wife, my chosen one and I want our marriage to be a good one again." I'll be back shortly, sweetie."

A STOP OFF AT TYRONE'S AND MONIQUE'S ROOM

....

Knock Knock---------Knock Knock Knock Knock Knock Knock. "Oh my gosh, Tyrone, get up its Lacy banging on the door." By this time Monique is already in a rage. "What's wrong with Imani, is she sick, maybe from that food she ate yesterday, maybe the two of you had a fight, did the two of you have a fight? Oh no, don't tell me this weekend failed, after all the work I put into it, come on come on why aren't you saying something, is Imani alright, and where is she?" "Monique, please, you had better cool down and wind down before you pass out. Baby, you're acting like a mad wild woman."

"Take it easy, Monique; everything's terrific with Imani and me. I am a happy married man. As a matter of fact, I stopped by your room to tell you that Imani and I will be staying in today. We have a lot to talk about and a lot of making up to do if we're going to resolve the issues we have been avoiding. However, we will be having dinner in the hotel's dining room and with you two if you don't mind joining us. I am on my way down to the dining room now to get breakfast for Imani and myself. We will see you two in the dining room for dinner, let's say around 6:00."

TOGETHER, JUST THE TWO OF US

....

"It feels so good talking over breakfast like this. I enjoy serving you breakfast in bed, just like before the twins were born. It seems like everything was done before the twins were born. Lacy, do you realize that you stopped being attentive to my needs after the twins were born? A woman wants the same needs met after the kids are born just as before the kids are born. Honey, our love was so strong we couldn't stand being apart back then and I felt so good loving you. I would like to experience that again." "So would I sweetie, it's left up to us to make things happen and I believe we both can put the past behind us and make our marriage and family a loving union again. The one thing that bothered me in a crazy way is the relationship with you and another woman, and I still find it hard to believe. Did I hurt you so bad that you couldn't stand the idea of me being with someone else, especially the thought of me in the arms of another woman? Imani, I am so ashamed and I am hurting about what I did to you. For me to feel this hurt I now know what you were going through because of my neglect to you as a husband."

"Lacy, we both have plenty unfinished business to take care of when we get back home. How do you think your lady friend is going to take it when you tell her that you can no longer see her because you are now my husband one hundred percent and it is goodbye for the two of you"? "Imani I feel uneasy about it and I pray that everything is okay." "You just remember my dear husband that you are a lawyer and you may have some work to do, so be prepared."

THE MIND OF A SCORNED WOMAN

....

Samantha Skye's mind is consumed with hate and all she can think about is revenge on Lacy Ball for making a fool out of her. He had her thinking that he was going to leave his wife and the two of them would be together. She fell in love with him and now she is hurting. She had built her dreams around Lacy Ball.

"I am going to make that man pay dearly for what he did to me. I am not going to rest until I see him down with nobody to go to for comfort as I am feeling now. Lacy Ball will regret the day he ever laid eyes on me. Right now, I feel nothing but hate for him. Just the idea of that man making love to his wife instead of me makes me sick."

THE DANGER ZONE

....

Samantha is making it her business to learn everything possible about the Ball twins, who are the children of Lacy and Imani Ball. It now seems like the dark side of Lacy's past is coming into the light and straight into his present life and home. The dark side always brings with it all Satan's warriors. OH BOY! When they band against the head of the household, they come in with a fierce satanic force that can destroy the whole family physically, mentally, and sometimes death. Samantha has moved from the stage of anger to the stage of madness. The demons have taken control over her.

"How would Mr. Lacy Ball like it if I kidnapped those twins of his? Just like he hurt me, I am going to hurt him. I want his heart to hurt the way my heart is hurting now. First I must learn his daily routine, his wife's daily routine, and the routine of his twin daughters including their school schedule. The Ball family will not have a clue as to what is happening until it is too late. I will stop by his office early Monday morning because he always stops by his office on Monday mornings to go over his schedule for the week and touch basis with his secretary just in case there have been changes that he needs to know about. I am going to be so nice to him. I will even give him a little bit while we are there in his office. My game is going to be so tight he will not suspect a thing concerning me. Hell, I will even help the family search for the twins and look as upset as the next person."

"The only reason that I have not told Monique about Tyrone and his client, who is also his lover, is because I don't want to hurt Tyrone. When I do get the chance, I will blow her mind with this juicy news. Right now, it's first thing first. I must take care of the Ball family first and the Haywill family will be on my back burner for a minute. Before I leave Detroit, I am going to make my mark. Everybody who crossed my path and did me wrong will feel the aftermath of Samantha Skye's horror storm. Yaaawn, yaaawn, I am so tired, I guess Planning, someone's doom is tiresome work."

....

The ride from the airport made Imani feel like she was coming back from her honeymoon. She and Lacy held hands all the way home. It was a good thing Tyrone was driving. Lacy and Imani has recaptured a love that has grown stronger than before. They are husband and wife and they are very much in love. It's like starting all over again and like they say, "things get better with age."

"Lacy, I have already told the babysitter that we need her to stay over one more night to be with Lacey and Stacey. She said that we got no important calls while we were gone. She said there was one strange call but she hung up on them. I think it was most likely a wrong number, but whatever it was about we can take care of it in the morning because I got big plans that includes only you and me. You were so attentive to my wants and needs while we were on Mackinac Island and now it is my turn to lay it on you. I don't want you to do anything for the rest of the night. I just want to love you, make love to you and bask in the warmth of your love. I don't want you to even lift your fingers to eat, I will feed you. I have been practicing in my mind how I am going to make love to you my dear sweet husband and you are going to get it and get it all night long but first, I am going to give you a sample right now." "Oh baby!"

BACK AT THE HAYWILL HOME

....

"Tyrone I really enjoyed this weekend. I feel good knowing our two best friends are back together, thanks to me for believing in them. I sure hope I never have to go through that with you. But I think you already know that I would have to kill you. Please don't make me kill you. I love you and I would miss you." "Monique, you should not tease that way because people may think you mean it." "What people, sweetheart, this is between you and me; and I will kill your black ass. Would you want to put it to a test to find out what will happen? The only thing is that you will never know what happened."

"Damn Tyrone, you look like you've seen a ghost. Do you think that I would harm you? I love and adore you. You are a part of me, and I need all of me to live. My dear sweet husband, without you there is no me. So I guess I will have to let you live, ha ha. Tyrone, please say something." "What do you expect me to say, and don't tell me you were joking because I know when you are joking with me Monique, and you were very serious about what you were saying." "Baby, what do I have to do for you to believe me when I say I love you, because I do love you, and I, think you know that. Why don't you let me give you one of my (just for my man) body massages like always. My special touch always put you in a state of relaxation." "You do not have to offer that twice, because baby, I am ready." Monique's thought is "you better be scared of me." The truth is, Monique doesn't know what she will do if Tyrone gets caught cheating.

After Tyrone's full body massage given to him by his wife, Monique, he relaxed for a couple of hours before they had their talk concerning Samantha Skye and how to handle the situation their best friends are faced with. "Monique, I have a feeling that all hell is going to break loose with Samantha. I don't think she will gracefully walk away from her affair with Lacy. I hope he is being careful and also keeping a watchful eye on his home front. I just don't trust Samantha." Monique always take notice how nervous Tyrone gets when discussing Samantha and her evil capabilities and the distance she will go to get what she wants.

"Tyrone, if there is something you want to tell me, please do so before I hear it from someone else. If you've been out there screwing around and Samantha knows about it, she will tell it. You will dance to the beat of her drums when it comes to her and Lacy. She will demand that you help her get Lacy away from his wife or she will tell your wife something that your wife has no clue about. Sweetheart, sometimes even when it might hurt, it is good to clear the conscious and disarm the person with all the ammunition that's gathered and aimed to destroy whoever is the target. The truth is it's the wife who always get hurt and that can destroy the whole family, so you better start talking and come clean while I am still sane and might be ready to forgive."

"Monique, I swear to you and if I had a bible right now, I would put my right hand on it to proclaim to you that I am telling you the truth. Baby I love you, and I know that you love me too. I would have to be crazy to do something stupid and destroy that love."

"I am going to talk to Lacy and try to convince him to stay as far away from Samantha as possible because she cannot be trusted. He needs to also have her barred from the office so there will be no close encounter with her. And baby, tell Imani to keep the home alarm on at all times and the car locked in the garage. It is better to be safe than sorry."

"Sweetheart, I will be talking with Imani about safety and also about us spending more time together at my boutique instead of her being at home alone writing. I know that she has a book to finish and I also know that she has been pushing herself to meet a deadline for the book she is writing. Maybe the two of us can put our heads together and come up with something that might work for her protection and get her out of the house at the same time. Why don't you and Lacy put your heads together and see what you guys come up with. This is teamwork consolidated."

....

"I must keep record of everything I learn about Lacy Ball and his family's whereabouts so that there will be no slip ups when I am ready to spring into action. Lacy made a big mistake when he played with my heart. The man will soon learn that when you play, you will damn sure pay. Samantha Skye is no free play, and she is now cashing in."

"I wonder what he is doing now. I bet his wife is in his arms and he is giving her those long passionate kisses the way he use to do with me. He is probably telling her how much he loves her and how much he enjoys their sex life. He probably can't get enough of her just as he was with me. The bastard should be with me right now, but instead he chose to go back to being a lover to his wife. Oh, how that Lacy is going to pay for what he has done to me. His whole family will pay and it is all his fault. I hate him so much I could kill him, but I need him to suffer first. When I'm finished with him he's going to wish he was dead. I must write my plans out before I act on them."

"It's early Sunday evening and if Lacy and Imani went away only for the weekend they should be back by now. I'll call Lacy and hear what he has to say to me now. No, I'll wait until tomorrow and call him at his office. If he goes straight to the courts, then I'll just plan to spend some time in his courtroom and sit where he will see my face and know that I'm there. I will be his nightmare until I am ready for action. I will visit his office, I will hang around inside the office building where his office is, and I will go to his favorite restaurant where he usually goes for lunch, not the one he always took me to on his lunchtime. Every time that man turns around he will see this gorgeous me."

MEANTIME BACK AT BROWN SUGAR'S BEAUTY SHOP

....

"I just can't believe that woman, Ms. Samantha, I'm calling her crazy Samantha because she is crazy as hell. She had the nerve to entertain the thought in that whopped mind of hers to talk me into harming my dear friend, Imani, the nerve of that crazy witch. I don't want Imani's marriage to go bad. Hell, we're just kick-around partners and it's been like that with us for years, since high school. Imani has not always lived on the hill away from us regular folks, as they like to call us in the hood, and her family just had a little ($change$) and could afford a big house outside the hood, that's all. The whole world does not need to know our business, and I am quite surprised that she opened that book on us. She comes to me when she needs a little sexual attention. There was no reason for her husband to know about us. As a matter of fact, she suspected her husband of having an affair. She knew that she couldn't stop it, so she turned to me because of our past relationship and she knew that I would also be here for her as a friend. Everything was kept between us two girls. Imani never had a desire to be with another man because she truly loves her husband, Lacy. If my girl doesn't call me real soon I am going to give her a call, whether Lacy is with her or not. She needs to know that Lacy's no good woman has plans to do her harm, and that she needs to watch her back. Legs, I am glad you came to work early and thank you for letting me ventilate my little problem on you. I could never have shared this with any of thc other girls around here. You are the only one who does not gossip around here. Legs, you are so smooth with your action without ever speaking a word. Girl, when I say you are good people and can handle your stuff, you just know it's okay if you come back at me with, "I'm all that and a bag of chips", girl, I ain't mad at you." There's one thing that buzzard should know and that is she cannot think that she can come into the hood and snap her pretty little finger and her demonic deeds will be done. Everybody's not dancing with the devil like herself."

MONIQUE VISITS IMANI

....

Monique shows up at the Ball's resident very tense and her voice showed urgency as she spoke to Imani. "Monique, what is it that you are rambling on and on about? I am in a hurry, I have somewhere I need to go this morning." "Imani I have to talk to you about something important and it cannot wait. Wherever it is you got to go I'm sure it can wait because what I got to say is more important and you're going to listen if I have to hold you down long enough for you to hear what I got to say." "Monique, I will give you thirty minutes to tell me what is so important that it can't wait for a more convenient time. Go ahead Monique, talk to me."

"Imani, why are you making this talk so hard for me? You know I wouldn't be here so early in the morning unless it is important. You're my best friend and I want you to have the best of everything that's good for you. So will you please sit down and relax your body because you are making me nervous with all that jumping around." "Monique, you are scaring me now. I've never seen you this nervous one on one with me before, I'm going to perk us a pot of coffee, and strong with caffeine just the way you like it." "Girl, let it walk to me." "Why don't we sit out on the patio and catch some of this outside morning breeze." And please, stop talking for a minute, just one little bitty minute."

As both Monique and Imani began to relax themselves, they delayed their talking while sipping their coffee and nibbling on the cheese toast Imani served to relax them while they talked. As Monique sipped her coffee she begin to think about how things used to be with the two of them. They had so much fun shopping for their husbands, picking out things that would look good on them or something for their office. When you walk into Tyrone's and Lacy's office, both offices show the Monique and Imani touch. The flawless cut diamond on their tie pins and cuff pins are their wives' special design, and they have them in several different designs and colors, from yellow gold, white gold, and the most expensive, the platinum design.

Monique is thinking about the times when they would discuss the things that they wanted to do for their love ones and they would plan according to their discussions over lunch or phone conversations, and often it would be done independently from habit and the love they have for their husbands.

Eleven

(Imani faces the truth)

....

As Imani and Monique sipped their coffee and ate toast they are in total silence just enjoying the early morning breeze. Detroit's summer mornings are always beautiful. A person feels beautiful just being out in the early morning breeze. "Well, I think it's time for the two of us to have that talk. Imani, I am not going to sugarcoat anything. As you already know, Lacy, your dear husband, has been seeing Samantha Skye. I think she came from Chicago, I'm not sure, but I do know that she didn't come from what we call Down South, maybe her folks did, from the bush, hich is a good place to be and just live off the land. Anyway, she was under the impression that Lacy was going to leave you for her. Tyrone and I think maybe it was her who called your home while we were away on Mackinac Island. Tyrone also said that he wouldn't trust her and that you should be careful because she may come with revenge on Lacy and his family. Because she thinks that she is so much in love with him, she may be looking at you as the other woman. I just want you to be careful, and if she is not up to anything, it is still good practice to be careful rather than sorry."

"Monique, I want you to look at me and tell me if you truly believe that my family is in danger." "Imani, I truly believe that there is a possibility that your family's lives are in danger by the hands of Samantha Skye. Brown Sugar has been trying to reach me by phone and I have not returned her call yet. Why don't you ride with me to her shop, maybe, she wants to apologize to me for kicking me out of her beauty shop last week. When we get back, I want to run a plan I have in mind across to you and then you can let me know what you think."

As Monique and Imani arrived in Brown Sugar's neck-of-the-woods (so-to-speak), "Well, I can see through the big glass window that Brown Sugar is still putting on a show for the people passing by her shop. She dresses skimpy even during the winter months when snow and ice is on the ground." "Well well, well, will you look at who just walked in. Good to see you Imani and you too,

Monique. Monique, is this a social visit or business, your presence caught me by surprise because I have been trying to reach you by phone with no success in return. I am glad Imani is with you, the three of us need to talk." "Brown Sugar, today it is business, the next time let's make it social." "Let's go to the back room so that we can have our privacy. We need to talk about that Samantha bitch, and I'm not saying it lightly. The woman is dangerous, and I am scared of her myself." As they walked while talking, Brown Sugar directed them to a table in the back room. "Let's sit here at the table and I will get cold drinks for us."

"Monique and Imani, the drama started early Monday morning when Samantha came to my shop to talk to me. I was surprised to see her here, and so early in the morning before I opened my doors for business. She said that she wanted to talk to me. Although I wondered why, I neglected to ask her the reason for the talk. Samantha quickly announced the reason why she was here to talk to me. Ladies I was in shock when she told me that she wanted me to get even with Lacy for going away with his wife for the weekend. I told her to get the hell out of my shop, and I didn't bite my tongue."

"My mind is made up Imani; you are going to spend your working hours with me. We will set up your computer at my boutique and you can do your writing there. The reason I can't let you use my computer is because I use my computer for my business. Even with an alarm in your home I don't trust you being there alone. I believe Samantha is capable of murder. There are evil spirit ways about her." I thank you ladies for being my friends, I appreciate all that you are doing, but I can't start running scared thinking that Samantha is trying to kill me."

"Brown Sugar, I am going to call you Ms. B, as always, it fits you and it gives you a little class, so you wear it girl, and you wear it well. Now we need to put our heads together and come up with something to do about Imani's safety. She's the same as always, she sees everything through rose color lens. Our friend doesn't seem to understand people at all. When the demon rises up far enough for you to see the head, it would be crazy to wait around for the whole body to materialize just for the sole purpose of destroying you and all that you claim as yours. Samantha Skye is like a wolf in sheep clothing, a demon straight out of hell, and Ms. B, it is left up to us to save the Ball family." "I am with you all the way Monique. I would simply die if anything should happen to Imani and her family. I have always supported Imani in her marriage to Lacy, it's just that our friendship went beyond the normal kind and we kept the secret so that no one would get hurt by gossip and all the other nasty things that the so-call-normal-people dish out at you. If Lacy opens up a little he might find out that he has a freak in bed. I bet that would blow his mind and his nuts too." "Ms B, I got news for you, Lacy already knows Imani is a freak in the bed, and I bet Lacy learned that he's got a freak and more, after that grand weekend on Mackinac Island. He probably was freaked out himself just taking it all in. I am sure that with him and Tyrone being good friends, they have talked about things that both men and women enjoy in sex. The poor man didn't know what he had at home, and now he has experienced both sides of his world, his wife at home and his bitch in the streets. Now that he doesn't have to go out to take care of those fantasies of his, he is finished with Samantha, and we all know that Samantha is not going to let it be. Let's put our heads together and come up with something that will get Samantha packed and running. Also, we must come up with what we need to do in order to keep our girl safe from that demon."

MEANTIME AT THE COURTHOUSE

....

Tyrone and Lacy just happened to meet in the hallway after coming from separate courtrooms. Tyrone suggested that they have lunch there at the courthouse because that would give them extra time to talk before they go back to court. There are things that Tyrone and Lacy should know about Samantha, and they need to talk now and more on the matter at another time with complete privacy. Their conversation is casual as they get on the elevator to go down. Lacy kept feeling uneasy about something, but he didn't know what it was. Tyrone noticed the way he was looking and asked him if there were anything wrong. "I will be going over my case, and I will do a double check and look at every single detail very carefully. Maybe there is something wrong there. This is someone's life that I am holding in the palm of my hands and I am going to make sure that I do everything I can possibly do to help my client. I can't think of anything else that would have my inner spirit in such an uproar."

"Lacy, my man, I am going to talk and you are going to listen, but first, let's get our food and find a table for two." "Tyrone, I see a table for two over at the window, while you are getting your lunch I'll go over and hold the table for us and then I will get mine." As the two men sat at the table to eat, and before Lacy and Tyrone could begin their conversation, there was about to be an interruption. "Man, I don't believe this." "Tyrone, what is the matter, why do you have that crazy mean look on your face?" As Lacy was talking he was turning at the same time to see what Tyrone was looking at. It was Samantha walking toward them. "Lacy, I will call you, and I want you to think about Mackinac Island."

If facial expressions could speak, Tyrone's face would have said with choice words, that Lacy should kill that bitch. Lacy needs to take her to a place of no return, and if I have to endure her interference much more, then I may be the one responsible for the annihilation of Samantha's Skye. Damn a man could get arrested and charged for murder just from his thoughts.

Tyrone has so many thoughts going on in his head. He knows that his main thought should be on his clients who need his undivided attention. All the mess that is going on in the life of the Ball's family has without a doubt moved on over into the life of the Haywill's family. Samantha may think that she is in the driver's seat but like all evildoers her road will come to an end and Samantha will get hers. Sooner or later she will either, give up and go running like a dog with her tail dragging between her legs or she will meet her maker by the hands of Lacy or someone close to the subject. Either way, Samantha Skye is headed in the right direction to meet her doom.

Twelve

(Back at Brown Sugar's Beauty Shop)

....

Monique and Brown Sugar are straining their brains to come up with the best plan for keeping Imani and her family safe from Samantha, the demon. Ms. B, why don't you go and make another pitcher of that great tasting ice tea, it looks like we may be here for awhile. Imani, I don't want you to say a damn thing about what we're trying to do to help you since you don't believe cat shit stinks. Here we are trying to come up with a good plan to save your ass from Satan's upscale demon, Samantha Skye, and you can't believe that she would do such a thing, hell woman, she has been screwing your husband. Do you have to see him insert it in her before you wake up and smell the coffee or in Lacy's case, Samantha's scent on his, ass. If she likes what she got with Lacy you can bet she will not be willing to let him go so easy, and I can't say it's all in her mind because I know better. Anyway, Lacy is not hers to have and she has to know that because he has a wife, you foxy lady."

"Here is that big pitcher of cold ice tea, now let's talk. Monique, have you told Imani to shut up and stay that way until it is time for her to speak." "Imani knows what's what, bottom line. What I have in mind is that Imani spends her days with me and do her writing at my boutique and there is plenty of space for her to work. There is a room that I have been using for storage that can be turned into an office for her. When she drops her daughters off to school she will come straight to my shop. Ms. B, it will be either you or me who will go with her to pick the twins up from school and then on to her house and stay there until Lacy gets home. It is very important that neither Imani nor the twins are left at home alone." "Monique, I think it is a great working plan."

"Now that you ladies have planned my life, may I speak?" "Yes Imani, please speak because we do need feedback from you." "Monique and Ms. B, I do appreciate what you ladies are doing for me and I am going to work with you, just tell me what to do. I have no reason to doubt you, because there is no way you would do all this unless my family was in a dangerous situation. Monique, I will spend today clearing your storage room and I will set up my computer equipment tomorrow. Will Tyrone be talking with Lacy about all we are doing"? "Of course, you know I would confide in my husband before taking on a task such as this one. My husband was ready and willing to help a brother out; after all, they are best friends and not just partners in the law firm. As a matter of fact, Tyrone will be talking with your husband today. Don't forget, the main ingredient here is, BEST FRIENDS. He will try to see Lacy today at the courthouse and set up a meeting for after work unless they can have lunch downtown between court appearances." "Imani, I can tell you right now that Ms. B and I wouldn't have it any other way. Talk with Lacy tonight and I will talk with you first thing in the morning. Ms. B, we are going to my boutique and get things started, and I want you to know that I will keep you updated with progress on the Ball family and that Ms. Bitch. By-the-way, it would be good to stop by my boutique sometimes, I have a nice line of clothes." "Not for me at your prices, good-bye ladies."

"Monique, I am so happy that you and Ms. B are getting along well with each other again. I know it is because of me, and to have both my friends together again makes me feel good. Monique, I have always wanted to tell you about Brown Sugar and me but I always thought that maybe you wouldn't understand me at all." "Imani, I still don't understand you. How in hell did you manage to get involved with Ms. B sexually anyway? Come on help me to understand because I sure as hell don't understand you going that way, and I am not criticizing you just because I do not understand you."

"I was with Ms. B at the time when I was feeling low and she did what a friend would normally do. She put her arms around me to comfort me". "I bet it did, go on tell me more." "It turned into a passionate kiss and before I knew it and before I realized what was taking place I was undressed and lying in her bed. It was an experience that blew my mind that night. A week later she called me to go shopping at the mall and to have lunch and just spend time together. Of course, we ended up back at her apartment having another sexual encounter. That time it was different because the two of us were not together to comfort me due to a low point in my life."

"Damn Imani, don't stop now, keep the story going, I am all ears with no interruption on my part." "Monique, I must say that on that day, Ms. B changed my whole world. She opened up sensitive areas of my body I did not know even existed. I experienced a total body sexual orgasm, and I have never had that with Lacy, not even on Mackinac

Island, if you know what I mean. Don't get me wrong now, because Lacy and I have always had good sex, but nothing like what I experienced with Brown Sugar, Ms. B as you like to address her. It was different from the time when we were teenagers and she introduced me to a sexual experience her way. She is an adult now and that woman has experience in sex that is unbelievable and just plain good." "Imani, what in the hell are you talking about? Did I just hear you say something about you, Brown Sugar and when we were teenagers? No, don't tell me because I am not ready to hear.

"Girl, your marriage has been in trouble since day one. Tyrone is going to have to teach Lacy a few things about a woman and her body, all of her body, every inch of it. I personally don't know what it feels like to not have a total body sexual orgasm. The problem with Lacy is that he has never brought the best out of you, which means that you have never delivered the best to him. Imani, you poor baby and to think, how selfish that man has been. I can understand now how Ms. B was able to get to you that way, and I still say that when a man does it up right there is no comparison. I know and I do love my husband."

LACY'S WORST LUNCH EVER

....

As Lacy sat and listened while Samantha did all the talking, he could not believe what was coming out of her mouth. She was letting him know with very clear sound and texture all her demands, and all that she will be expecting of him from now on. He was sitting there with a stupid look on his face wandering if she was really serious about her plans and threats. Lacy mumbled softly under his breath "this woman is damn crazy." He also realized the danger she posses in her mind, and that his family is in her plan to be the recipient of that danger. Lacy cannot help but think about the danger he has put his family in, and it is all because of the dog in him, and right now he can't even recall the so call big thrill from it. His thoughts are, "what a big waste and it could cost me my whole family." He has to think of something to get out of this bad situation. "I need some time alone." Lacy knew how important it was for him to be alone. He had a lot of soul searching to do and a whole lot of accountability to own up to before asking for forgiveness". After ending his lunch time with Samantha, Lacy hurried to his private place.

"Dear Heavenly Father, I know that I have not been right in my life, and God, I know that I have wronged my family because your commandments tell me your expectations of me as man on this earth. You said thou shall not commit adultery, and I did. Lord I come to you on bending knees asking you to please have mercy on my family. Dear Lord, if you will please forgive me for my wrong doing, I promise you that I will live the life that is expected of me as your child here on earth. Your Son, Jesus, died on the cross so that you will forgive my sins. He knows my weakness as my Heavenly Father knows them also. I am praying to you in Your Son, Jesus name, Amen."

Lacy knows that he has plenty to atone for but none as major as what he has put upon his loving family. Crazy thoughts are rambling around in his head and he can't seem to shake them loose. One thing for sure is that when he sees Samantha he does not look at her with a sexual desire anymore. All he can feel for her at this time is contempt with a desire to kill her. "I don't know what I was thinking about to contemplate the thought of leaving a beautiful Christian woman like my wife, Imani for a Jezebel like Samantha. I was not dealing with a full deck at the time. I know I wasn't because there is no way I would have chosen that woman over my wife. A man dealing with a full deck would never give up an eighty plus for a twenty minus." No matter how Lacy tries to put it, none of it makes sense, yet he keeps beating up on himself.

Lacy begins to have flashbacks full of good memories about early on when he first met Imani and all the fun they use to have with Tyrone and Monique. For him life was beautiful back then. He had met and was dating a beautiful woman who was well educated with financial means of living a good life. She enjoyed writing and he enjoyed reading her transcripts, as a matter of fact he loved her work and anticipated reading it. The one memory he will forever keep close to his heart and that is, the very first time he and Imani made love. He knew at that time he wanted her to be his wife because he felt a spiritual connection. She had great writing skills with a business mind, she had money, she had and still has beauty and she is smart enough to know how to keep her man happy. "Starting today, I am making a change in my life and I believe my family will appreciate and welcome the change."

(Dinner time at the Ball's Mansion)

....

The twins are surprise to see their father at home for dinner. His appearance at dinnertime has been rare. "Daddy, why are you home so early?" "Baby girl, I have been missing you and your sister Stacey so much that I have made up my mind not to let anything come between my family and me because you are the most important part of me. Daddy will keep his promise to you that unless there is a dying emergency, I will be having dinner with my girls and that includes your mother, my beautiful big girl."

"Stacey, and you too Lacey. I want you to know that I have a surprise waiting for your father in the master bedroom and he does not know what the surprise is. The reason I am telling you this is that you may hear a scream coming from our bedroom and I don't want you to become alarm. The surprise I have for him may take him by surprise. By all means girls, do not get out of bed because you think something is wrong. I was thinking how nice it would be for the four of us to play the game of monopoly after dinner the way we use to do when Tyrone was coming home early and we played that game and other family games. I want to keep your daddy guessing what his surprise might be."

Lacy, Monique and their girls are having so much fun playing their favorite board game. Each twin is teamed with one of their parents and the game is so heated up to the point of making fun at the team that seems to be losing. There are lots of laughing and playing around which makes the whole scene of the game fun, fun, and more fun. After about an hour, Monique broke the game up because it was getting late and she wanted everybody to start getting ready for bed. She wanted everybody up bright and early tomorrow morning because of the daily change of her normal routine. Imani will be going to Monique's Boutique and using Monique's computer to work on her novel. "I must remember to bring my memory stick with me to transfer information back to my computer at home."

"Lacy, for old time sake, will you please take the dishes from the dishwasher and put them away, and I'll be in the master bedroom waiting for you." "Imani, I hope you have not been out spending big bucks on me. I know that you like your man looking good and well dressed, but baby don't you think your man already represents in a way that is to your taste, and baby you know that you represent like the queen you are. You are a beautiful black woman and you're my beautiful black woman."

Lacy does not know it but he is in for a surprise he is no way close to expecting. While Lacy was busy in the kitchen, Imani was getting ready for him in the bedroom. After Lacy finished in the kitchen he went to the bedroom to join his wife and as he opened the bedroom door, Imani, wearing next to nothing heard his footsteps and was standing on the other side of the door with her hands extended with two glasses of champagne in them. Lacy was in shock, and at the same time he could not keep his eyes off her. The classic song, "Have I Told You Lately That I Love You" was playing softly on the CD and the music consumed the room. Lacy took a sip from his glass before putting it down and he pulled Imani close to him. He held her lovingly in his arms and kissed her softly on her lips and they began to dance to the song that was playing. They held each other in their arms for a little while before going to bed.

THE MORNING AFTER

....

"Imani baby, you are the most magnificent woman a man could ever dream of having in his life. Last night was a night that I will never forget. I can't imagine myself happier than I am right now. I know that I am a blessed man because the happiness we share has to be heavenly divine." "Sweetheart, I know you love me and I want to please you in every way a wife could possibly please her husband in return." "You do please me. I am happy with you."

Knock, knock, knock. "Mama, daddy, can we come in and see daddy's surprise, we heard the noise when you gave it to him and he was really surprised too. Can we come in and see it?" "No, you can't come in. Your daddy and I will see you girls at the breakfast table, and will one of you please plug in the coffee pot for me so that the coffee will be perked when I come to the kitchen." "Come on Stacey, it's probably an ugly shirt she bought at the mall, and his screams were the horror of knowing he's got to wear the ugly thing."

"Lacy, please don't let them hear you laughing." "I can't help it baby, ha, ha, ha, ha, ha, ha, ha, ha, I can't stop, ha, ha, ha, ha, I can't help it." "Lacy I am going to put a towel in your mouth, stop laughing." "Baby I have never had a day like this since we've been married, and just think, it is still early morning. I love this family. I am a happy man, ha, ha, ha, ha, ha, ha."

"Lacy, I will get breakfast ready and will you please drop the girls off at school, and of course I will pick them up after school. We will be a little late today because the girls have their piano lessons after school."

Thirteen

Buzzzzz, buzzzzz, buzzzzz, buzzzzz. "Good morning Monique, you are here very early. I was not expecting you so early. Lacy just left to take the girls to school before going to his office. He said something about a late court appearance so maybe he will get a chance to talk to Lacy. I have a pot of hot brewed caffeine coffee perked and ready to be consumed, come on in the kitchen and join me. This is my second cup but I have not had breakfast yet. There is plenty left because Lacy and the girls were not very hungry this morning. You can sit and sip your coffee while I heat the food."

"This gives me a chance to tell you about Lacy and me, also about the oneness the two of us experienced last night." "Girlfriend, I thought there was a special kind of glow about you this morning. I am all ears and I want to hear everything, details, details, details." All I can say is that man gets better and better every time. Every time I lay one on him he delivers back with pure delight. I can't believe I considered walking out on all this good stuff, and I mean Good stuff with a capital G. He knows how to make love to me. I think I'll play a little bit of Gerald Levert and reminisce about last night." "Just like a newborn baby, you're experiencing everything for the first time in a great height of multiples. I'm surprised you didn't almost blackout. I know I almost did once upon a time when Tyrone had every sensuous nerve throughout my body working at the same time, from my toes to my fingertips straight to my head. I better get these thoughts out of my head, we got work to do." "Monique, I must say, I liked it, no I loved it. I know that your husband has been schooling my husband. Thanks for telling him about what I told you."

A DAY AT THE BOUTIQUE

....

"Monique, this is a nice room that you are giving up for me to work on my novel. I am almost finished with this book. Just imagine this is my fifth book and all my other books have sold well. If you need me for anything, you may pull me from my computer at anytime. Otherwise, I will be sitting quietly at my computer out of your way. I know that this is your place of business but I must give the boutique's number to a couple of places for immediate contact in case they can't reach me on my cell phone, such as my twins and my publisher. Of course it would be automatic for my husband. He will most likely talk to you instead of me if he is just calling to check up on me because he will want to hear from you that all is well with me."

"Monique, I know you want to know how things got started with me and Brown Sugar, and I want to tell you everything. It's a long story but I will give it to you in a summary type way."

"As soon as I open the entrance door to the boutique, we can start talking, and we can talk until the customers start coming in. I tell you Imani, Tyrone is still trying to figure this one out. Lacy knew that he had to get back, because there was no way he was going to go down like that. A man's ego will not accept the fact that it is possible for a woman to make love to another woman and satisfy her sexually as good or even better than a man can. What the husband has to realize is that it is not about love, but all about the flesh and all the desires it craves. So while the man is out there playing around, such as Lacy for an example, and his wife is at home cleaning and taking care of their children, he had better think twice about the word neglect. That girlfriend that she has over so often or go shopping with or go on trips with calling it a girlfriend's weekend away from home can also mean close encounter of the same gender. A good lay is a good lay no matter who is performing."

THE WELL KEPT SECRET

....

"Monique, we grew up together, and it seems as though we have always known each other because all during our childhood days we were together. It was when we started high school that something happened that changed my life from the norm to one big secret. The two of us met Brown Sugar at the same time, but she grew closer to me for some reason." "And we both know that reason don't we?" "Do not interrupt me Monique, I am telling you a story of my life."

"It was summer after ninth grade when your parents took you away on vacation. Brown Sugar came over and we spent the day together. We had a great time talking, and she asked me about my experience with boys. Of course you know I was a virgin back then, which surprised her. She told me that she was not a virgin and she went on to tell me about how good it felt to have someone to make love to her. She knew that she had gotten my attention then, and she continued to talk, telling me things in details. When she asked me if I wanted to know how it feels, I told her no, and that I was not going to let a boy do that to me. I told her that my mother and my father would kill me if they found out that I let a boy do that to me. She said to me that she could show me and it wouldn't cause any harm because we are both girls. I was so naïve, I fell for it." "And you're still naïve about people and some things." "There you go interrupting me again. Monique, will you please shut up and let me finish my story." "I will finish your story right now for you. One big story rolled up in a nut shell goes like this,……You did it, you liked it, and you continued it,……bottom line with story told and finished."

SAMANTHA'S BIG PLAN IS UNFOLDING

…………………………………………………

Samantha seems to be full of hate for people who she believes did her wrong by coming between her and Lacy. She is consumed with hate to the point that she has become capable of killing another person. All she can think about is revenge. Somebody is going to pay for the hurt she is feeling, and there is no easing of the pain, and the hurt gets worst each day. She is thinking that somebody will pay in a big way for her hurt.

As Samantha sits at her kitchen table, sipping coffee with a shot of bourbon in it, she is caught up in thought of what she will do to carry out her plan. "I am going to kidnap Lacy's twin girls. He said that his twin daughters were his life, so I am going to take his life." Samantha then started putting her plans on paper. She bought a notebook just for that occasion.

"I am going to write down everything that I need to do, step by step to make my plan work. I will watch the twins' daily routine and also the daily routine of Lacy and Imani. Lacy has already told me that his wife spends most of her day at home writing. She would be an easy pick but she is not the one I want. I just want to know her whereabouts so I can carry out my plan to snatch the twins. As for Lacy, all I need to know is that he is tied up in court all day. As far as Monique is concerned, I'll just wait until she goes away to do her buying for her boutique. That Brown Sugar is another story and may present a problem for me. I already know that she knows the kind of people who could and would keep an eye on me without me knowing about it. It doesn't mean that she knows only shady people but that she doesn't associate herself with only one stereo type person. That woman can hang with anybody, from the lowest in the bend stock to the highest of the crop. And she thinks that she is all that, and some. This bourbon is giving me a buzz; I think I better put down this cup of coffee." Samantha continues to be in deep thought.

THE DAILY PLAN

....

Monday..........Get a rental or leased car.
Tuesday..........Park nearby the school and check the time of the twin's arrival & departure.
Wednesday......Park near the Ball's home and make note of the full day routine.
Thursday.........Repeat Wednesday's routine.
Friday.............Visit the church the Balls attend every Sunday morning.

I will go over my notes and make all necessary changes and then repeat my routine plans. I will continue until I get the twins alone. I may have to get a job working at their school. Nobody will ever believe I will take on a nonprofessional job, but I can't be a teacher at their school because a teacher must be certified at their school. Well, I must get my rest now because Monday my whole life will change." Samantha thought about the job in which she has plans to apply for at the twins' school. She thought about the time she worked as a School Service Assistant when she lived in a suburban area in the State of New York. She is thinking that maybe the suburban schools near the metropolitan areas are pretty much the same as suburban New York. For the short time that she will need the position she will have the job done before her probation period is over anyway.

Fourteen

"Lacy, my man, I'm glad I ran into you." "Tyrone, I must apologize for that terrible lunch interruption with Samantha. I am free now, as a matter of fact, I am free for the rest of the day, what about you?" "I am free also, but I don't want to take the chance of running into Samantha again, so let's go someplace away from downtown." "That's good thinking, name a good place." "What about us meeting at Beans and Cornbread out on Northwestern Highway in Southfield." "Beans and Cornbread it is. I will meet you there in one hour. I need to stop by my wife's boutique first to see her about something."

AN HOUR LATER AT BEANS AND CORNBREAD

"Lacy, I just left your wife. Did you know that she had made plans to spend time with Monique at her boutique? She said that she wasn't sure that she had talked with you about the change in her daily routine schedule as to where she would spend her days finishing her transcript. She plans to have her novel in the book stores very soon. She said that she will ask your approval when she sees you tonight, otherwise she will stay at home. She asked me had we talked, and Lacy, we must talk today about this business with Samantha. Your family's safety is at stake. By the way, your wife has a glow on her face I have never seen before, ha, ha, ha."

"As a reminder, Lacy, your family has been invited to have dinner at my home this evening. If it's okay with you, I told my wife and your wife that I will bring home dinner from this restaurant. Monique also wants me to bring home a couple bottles of red wine. Just in case she forgot I think I should stop at the deli and get her favorite snack tray she likes with red wine."

"I just love the old Motown sounds they play at this restaurant. It always works up my appetite. I already know what I want, and I will ask for extra sweet potato muffins as I always do when I eat here. I see the waiter looking this way and I am ready to order, what about you?" "I am ready to order also." "I will have them put the takeout on hold until we're finished eating and having our talk and we can also continue our talk later after dessert with the wives input on decisions we know must be made concerning everybody's safety and wellbeing."

LET'S TALK SAMANTHA SKYE

....

"Tyrone, that woman, Samantha what's her name, is making my life a living hell. She told me that I will regret the day I chose my wife over her. She comes into the courtroom and just sits there and stares at me. I have even seen her parked across the street from my home. My wife is afraid to let Lacey and Stacey out to ride their bicycles. Tyrone, I am a lawyer and I can't even help myself. I am calling on you now as a friend, please tell me what it is I can do to stop this woman, short of killing her, and I have thought about that too."

"Lacy, I know that you are worried about your family, and I am worried too, and so is Monique who by the way saw through Samantha and started her own investigation and that is how I got involved. The reason Imani is at the boutique is because Monique doesn't trust her being alone at home and not knowing Samantha's where-a-bouts. We must remember that Samantha is very hurt. It is a possibility that she did fall in love with you. That is the danger of a married man having a sexual relationship with another woman. With us men, it is all about a sexual release by way of the penis with something a little different from with the home front, but with a woman it may mean a relationship that might go someplace, when you know damn well it ain't going no damn place as long as home front stays in place. Samantha has given up her most inner precious part of herself that should be honored and respected. Right now, I'm sure she feels used and misused. Us men can get up, shake it off and walk away, but the woman may feel attachment with the hope of a commitment in marriage for her future. Adultery is a trip to nowhere but down, both, physical and mental, and Samantha is feeling deeply hurt. Don't forget, the trick of the trade. almost pulled you away from home. Think about how miserable your life would have been without your family. When the good times are over, where do you go from there, my friend, except home, and the other person is left alone and destroyed."

"Tyrone, this wide awake nightmare is all because of the dog in me. I'm afraid that I have made a mistake that could destroy my whole family. My life is no good without my family, so how could I have done this to them?" "Lacy, don't beat up on yourself, and if you really want to hear the truth, I can lay that on you right now. You met this fine woman and all you could think about was how to lay her. Am I right so far, Mr. Lover Man? Don't answer me because I know the answer to that too. When you got the chance to get what you wanted, you found out that you were not with an amateur.

Samantha performed on you and with you like you had never had before. Am I still on target with this conversation? Don't answer me again. The lady had game and you had jack. How am I doing so far Mack Daddy? You were ready to leave your wife for her because you didn't want it to stop and, if she had been one of those back alley women happy with a little bit of your time just for a roll in the sack you would be living in two worlds, yours and hers. I know that I am still on target so I will go ahead and finish the story." "You're in the driver's seat and are heading home, so keep going, my brother."

"While on Mackinac Island you discovered that Imani could deliver just as good, and with some of it even better, or shall I say mmmmmmmgood. I know it happened because Monique and I went up to your room and before we could knock we heard some deep gut sounds of moaning and groaning. Imani was whipping your ass. It must have been like giving you a dessert, whipping her ingredients to perfection, so I know you shed some tears. I've been there, (Lord have mercy have I been there!) Don't feel bad about something that was that good to you. You were in your rights because you were with your wife. It happened to me, and from what Monique put on me, I would gladly do it again. The best tears a man could shed, and know that his ass's been whipped."

"Man, we got distracted for a moment and we do need to stay focused on what is most important. Samantha being in the courtroom may be a good thing for you Lacy; as a matter of fact it is good for all of us. When we know where she is, we will know that she is not out there trying to do harm to your family. You should feel pleased that she is where you can keep an eye on her. Lacy, by all means never drop your guard where that woman is concerned. I don't think your family will be safe until she leaves town. I think Monique's plan is a good one. "You're right; I will talk to our security staff and describe Samantha to them so that they can keep an eye out for her. She shouldn't be cruising through my neighborhood. It is not like she just turned off a street onto my street. She has to travel up through an exclusive area to get near our home." Once this is over, you should never even look at another woman twice. As a matter of fact, when this is over, you should drop to your knees and beg your wife to forgive you for being a big fool, and you must humble yourself and ask God to forgive you for your sin. Have you stopped to ask your Heavenly Father to put a protection shield around you and your wife and daughters? I don't go to church but I do know where my blessings come from, and after all that is happening, I think it is time for you to follow your wife on Sunday mornings."

"Tyrone, I am glad we had this talk. You have really been a crutch for me. If it were not for yours and Monique's plan for a trip to Mackinac Island, I would not be at home with my wife. I could never repay you for what you have done for Imani and me, and that includes Monique too." "Lacy, my man, all I can say is, the next time you feel that you need something different from what you have at home I want you to put a jacket on it and go pay for it where it is organized. Do what the rich boys do, and when you have finished you can just walk and never have to look back. And remember your wife is open to learn more about how to please you. She proved that to you on Mackinac Island." Lacy couldn't do anything but laugh, ha, ha, ha, ha, ha.

"I think the takeout is ready so we should leave for my house, our wives should already be there. I need to make a stop at the office before I go home so will you please take the food with you and tell Monique, I will be there in about an hour. Tell her that she can call the office if she needs anything for me to pickup while I am out, and let her know that I will be picking up the two bottles of red dry wine, that she wants."

Tyrone went straight to his office building and before he could get on the elevator he got a big surprise. Standing in the entrance nearby was Samantha, just looking and smiling at him. Lacy was dumbfounded by what he was seeing, and he was also wondering how she got passed the guard, unless she signed in and lied about why she was there in the building after working hours. The cleaning people are coming in, but Samantha is not dressed the part. Maybe she is pretending to be the supervisor for the cleaning crew.

"Samantha, why are you here and what, do you want at this late hour because all the offices are closed. Woman why are you standing there staring at me like something is seriously on your mind?" "I know what's going on; have fun." Samantha disappeared just as quickly as she appeared. It was like she was never there.

AN EVENING AT THE HAYWILL MANSION

....

"Imani, our children are really enjoying themselves. I can tell by the way they are laughing and making joyful noise, and I am enjoying myself too. Lacy you have been here for more than an hour and you said that Tyrone told you he was going to his office and to tell me that he will be at home in about an hour. I am going to call his office."

Rrrring, rrrring, rrrring, rrrring, rrrring, click. "I will now call his cell phone." Rrrring, rrrring, rrrring, rrrring, rrrring, click. His voice mail came on. One of these days, I will find out what he is doing when I cannot reach him." "Monique, I have the table all set and the children should be hungry by now, so I am going to pull them away from their playing so they can eat".

"I know that I am quite famished, what about you?" "My stomach has been rumbling for the past hour and that husband of mine is not home yet. I am very upset and whatever Tyrone is doing and whoever he is doing it with I will find out. When I do catch up with them I am going to let them have it in plain unsophisticated ghetto style beat down and they better pray that I don't turn the barrel around. I refuse to have another woman all up in my stuff. It's mine and I will not share my stuff with another woman."

"You ladies do not have to wait for Tyrone to come home before you eat your dinner. Tyrone and I had an early dinner at the restaurant where your dinner came from. Monique, Tyrone knows that you like the food at Beans and Cornbread that is why he decided on that particular restaurant. He also said that he would have the dry red wine you ask for, with him when he comes home. You know there has to be a good reason for him being late coming home. If I were you I would be a little worried about his safety instead of thinking he might be with another woman. I really didn't want you to worry but he did have a bad encounter with Samantha in the courthouse cafeteria a few days ago. If you want, I will go look for him, of course the office is the only place I know to go because that is where he said he was going".

Rrrring, rrrring, Monique grabbed the phone very quickly. "Hello Tyrone." "No, this is not Tyrone, but I did see him at his office building. All of you can run but you can't hide. I can get into wherever I want to and whenever I want to, click." "I don't believe this. That woman said that she saw Tyrone at his office building. What has she done to my husband?" "Calm down Monique, I am leaving right now for the office and if I am not back within the next two hours, call the police and tell them what happened." Just as Lacy was pulling out of the driveway, Tyrone pulled up. "Tyrone, where have you been?" We are all worried about you."

"Why, would you be worried about me, I told you where I was going and I know that I am a little late but that doesn't give cause to worry."

"Samantha just called and she gave us reasons to believe something was wrong. Where, have you been all this time?" "I was trying to tail Samantha in my car but she caught on to me and gave me the slip, so I went back to the office to take care of something for tomorrow morning." "Monique will be happy to see that you are safe." Tyrone was thinking, how lucky can a man get. "That lie fell right in place. I know I got to go to church."

Fifteen

A continued evening of entertainment with the Haywill family

……………………………………………………………

"Tyrone, since you and Lacy have already had your dinner, you men can have dessert and coffee while Imani and I have our dinner. Tyrone, I have your favorite desserts, apple pie with whipped cream and sweet potato pie with whipped cream, our favorite kind, REDDI WHIP. Lacy, Imani told me that those were your favorite desserts too. You can see that we are thinking about our husbands all the time."

"I bet you ladies would not be able to guess what Tyrone and I have planned for our wives. Why don't we play charade and find out. Tyrone you can go first." Monique and Imani anxiously waited for the game to begin and they are all into it. "Tyrone, you're moving your hands like you're swimming, does that mean we're going to the beach? No, then why are you moving your hands like you were gliding, are we going on an airplane someplace, no wait you're paddling a canoe, that's it we're going canoeing. Imani, we're going to Northern Michigan or maybe Canada, I love it." "Wrong again, Monique, why don't you give Imani a chance to guess at it." "Why don't you just tell me and stop this old stupid game." "Monique, with Lacy in and around water I would guess we are going on a cruise." Both men burst into a big laugh. "Imani baby, I am taking you where I can show you off. I am taking you on a cruise to Hawaii. I want to have in Hawaii what we had on Mackinac Island. My lady soul, I crave your kind of love. It is pure with peace and tranquility. I also got us a room on the ship with a balcony. Baby this will be our second honeymoon. This is my way of saying I love you." "Don't forget about Monique and me. We will also be on that ship sailing to Hawaii."

"Enough of all this sweet-talking-stuff, I just gained five pounds taking it all in. Let's talk about Chuckey's Grandma, the woman from hell. Sweetheart, how did she get into your office building? I thought building management had security in the lobby and throughout the whole building. I know they don't have just one guard covering all that building." "Monique they had to cut back on staff and that left only two guards left to cover the building, but we also had more cameras installed."

"Baby, I don't think anybody can stop that woman from doing what she set her mind to do. I had walked across the lobby to the elevator and before the door opened she appeared out of nowhere. She accused me of scheming to keep Lacy away from her. She said that I would pay for coming between her and Lacy. Baby, that woman is sick. Imani, you must also be careful because she believes in her sick mind that if it weren't for you she would be with Lacy, never mind you being his wife. Everybody listen up, it is important that we not discuss the cruise with anybody, not even our children. I would hate to be out there on the ocean and discover that she is on the same cruise ship as us."

"Why don't we partner up and play a few hands of bid whiz. Imani, are you ready to whip Monique and Tyrone like the last time we played? Let's play for a bigger stake this time, as a matter of fact let's see how deep our partners can dig. Let's go for a full evening starting with the new play that is coming to the Music Hall Theater, and afterward, dinner at one of Detroit's fine restaurants and from there drinks and entertainment at our favorite jazz club. Will you losers be able to handle that?" "We were losers last time, and the answer to your question is yes we can handle it and we are game, so let the game begin. Give me a kiss baby, I feel like a winner. You so call bragging former winners, if you are caught cheating, you then forfeited the game and that will make you the losers. I hope you've got a thousand dollars or more to spend that evening and it will be a long evening and plenty money spent, and the Haywills do not intend to lose this time."

As the card game begins everyone is nervous and the bidding is heating up. It looks like they are playing for blood tonight. Husband and wife team against husband and wife team, but, will they remain friends afterward. They decided on five games and the winning team must win three out of five games to win. Silence has fallen on the room where the game is being played and there's deep concentration on each face. When will the silence end?

"Honey, I don't feel good about what we're doing. We're supposed to be having a pleasant evening together, but there is nothing pleasant about this game." "Imani honey, I feel the same way. I think it is time for us to go home, go get the twins." "No, wait you two, this competition in a card game is just stupid. It is not worth us being uncomfortable this way. We all are worth more than a thousand dollars, and to think we are getting into a fighting match to prove something that is not important and it could break up our friendship." "Tyrone, please make them stay." "Monique has done it again, opening that big mouth of hers and saying what I had planned to say. Thanks baby, we always think alike." Tyrone spoke with an amusing smile on his face.

The Haywill family and the Ball family had lost track about why they have come together in the first place. They had quickly forgotten all about Samantha's revenge. They can count their blessings for such a strong friendship. They had almost let a bet, something as simple as a card game wage on who is better or best at playing cards destroy a lifetime friendship. It was not about the money because they both are wealthy men.

"Hey, everybody listen up, I, the one and only, Tyrone Haywill, has a great idea that we all will love." Lacy spoke quickly, "go on Tyrone, speak up, let us have it, we're listening." Suddenly everyone was silent. Tyrone spoke, "why don't we plan a celebration for Imani's recent published book while we are aboard the ship." Monique blurted out, PERFECT! "Lacy my man, we now have something to plan for and all the women have to do is be present and look pretty. We men will be the ones who will be spending the money on this special occasion." "Imani, my boutique has all the fine sexy clothes we need for the trip. Why don't you and I pick up a couple bottles of champagne and lock ourselves in my shop for a couple of hours to do some shopping for our cruise." "How much money am I spending, Lacy?" "For you Imani, all you want, since I know that you are a well managed shopper."

"Imani, it is getting late, why don't we go and get my girls while Lacy fetch the car. Monique and

Tyrone, this has been a pleasurable night and I think we accomplished a lot tonight. The next meet will be at our home. I will let Imani know so she can whip up some of her favorite dishes for us. "My buddy, I'll just say good night and go bring the car around to the front entrance, tell Imani to meet me there." "Lacy my man, until next time." "Gotcha buddy."

On the way home, Imani thought about how tonight reminded her of their former times together and how great it feels to recapture that again. "Lacy, tonight was so great, we forgot all about that she-devil, Samantha Skye." "We didn't exactly forget about her, we just put her on the back burner for a moment. Imani, we can't let that woman consume our lives, and we will deal with her. After tonight, I am 100% sure that the woman is dangerous and she is acting like an insane person." "With all this happening, why did you agree with Tyrone's idea and make this sudden decision to take a cruise?" "I believe being out of sight may cool Samantha's temper and allow her to see where she is going wrong with her thinking as for, as I am concerned. Our children, both families, will spend a couple of weeks on a farm in Alabama with my brother and his family. My brother and his wife, Floryjean, have two boys around the same age as our children. To make things even better, his wife's mother lives on the farm with them. Our kids will be with a family of three generations, now can you get any better than that? I will call my brother and his wife first thing tomorrow morning. Tyrone's idea for this cruise is looking better all the time." "I think so too baby, I think it is a good thing for us all. We need to get away and cool our heads. I will tell Tyrone and Monique about my plans for the children while we are away on the cruise, I'm sure they will agree with me." "Lacy, I love you." "I know, and back at you."

SHOPPING SPREE AT MONIQUE'S BOUTIQUE

Monique and Imani shop for the cruise

Monique and Imani meet at Monique's Boutique to pick out clothing for their cruise. "Imani, I picked up two bottles of champagne and it is on ice chilling. I also put together a cheese and cracker tray with a variety of cheese and crackers to go with our champagne." "Great, I am going to enjoy this shopping spree. Lacy is enriching your clothing sales big time in a matter of two hours." "Imani, my sales for you is as always, 50% for everything you purchase." "Monique, I feel like you're giving the clothes to me." "I am, 50% off, ha, ha, ha, ha, and don't forget about the shoes and purses, they're 50% off too."

"Imani, we're going to be the finest dressed women on the ship. I don't think our husbands will let us out of their sights." "I don't know about you, Monique, but I am going to make this trip a real second honeymoon. The last trip we all had together was good because we were able to get back as husband and wife, which is something we're still working on, but that crazy woman is not making it easy. Samantha has our lives in an uproar and Lacy is still blaming himself. I have told him that I forgive him and I know he believes me but the craziness has our lives in a bad state. Lacy and I wish the woman would just disappear out of our lives, but she just won't go away." "Imani, why don't we ease our minds about that woman, and let our husbands take care of everything. Men are better at handling certain situations, especially dangerous ones."

After trying on clothing and shoes, the two ladies made their choices of clothing with matching shoes to pack for the cruise. "Monique, this has been a busy shopping morning for me, and I enjoyed it. I'm now ready to relax with a snack and a glass of champagne." "I'm ready for a little something to snack on also. First, let's make a toast to ourselves just for the heck of it. Let's put ourselves on top for a change."

QUIETLY LEAVING THE STATE OF MICHIGAN
(Stop off in Alabama / Destination Florida)

Tyrone rents a large size vehicle and with his family packed and aboard he goes and picks up the Ball family. The trip departure time was scheduled for 4:00 a.m., because they wanted to be on the road by 5:00 a.m. in case Samantha came prowling later at the time the Balls would be leaving for work and school. Imani will make the call from her cell phone to the twin's school to let them know that they will be out for a couple of weeks. Monique will make the same kind of phone call to her kid's school. The kids fell asleep and didn't wake up until they stopped for late morning breakfast. The road trip was beginning to be a fun trip. The kids were laughing at the grown-ups crazy jokes and they all joined in singing along with the radio. They kept it up until it was time to stop for lunch. By that time they were almost in Georgia and closer to Alabama.

Lacy spoke first, "Well, everybody we're here and all we have to do is head for the countryside and within less than an hour we will be at my brother's farm. They are expecting us and I know they will have a full course dinner ready for us. Everybody get ready, for some down-home-cooking Alabama style."

Ty, Jr. spoke first, "look at all the trees around that house. I am going to have a good time climbing on those limbs." "Cool it, my beautiful bird, there will be no tree climbing, do you understand me, young man." "Yes daddy."

"Lacy, there is someone waving to us from the barn over there." "That's my brother, Spencer. "Imani, don't you remember him, he was at our wedding, but he wasn't married at that time." "Yes, now I remember, he wasn't as big, back then, especially in the middle, but I can see the face is the same." "Imani, I heard that his wife is a good cook and she believes in the family eating a full course freshly cooked meal every day." "Lacy, I guess I'm just a city girl with city ways, I like to write, shop, and look pretty for my husband, is there something wrong with that?" "No, I love you just the way you are, and I also want to know if you are trying to start an argument with me." "No, I'm not, but you seem to suddenly have a problem with me as your wife and what I do or not do and I can't stand that kind of comparison." "Imani, I love you just the way you are."

"Imani, they're beckoning for us to join everybody at the house, I think it is time for us to eat dinner." "Yes, let's go in so that we can enjoy our family and eat with them." Monique and Tyrone had already made themselves acquainted with the family. The kids were already playing together and having a ball. Soon everybody was called to the dinner tables. There were three tables pushed together so all will be able to eat together and enjoy in good talk. The adults even told a few jokes to give the kids something to laugh about. Everyone was included in the good eating and talk. There was something about the food that gave the sense of being prayed over before cooking and, Floryjean cooked with love and to top that off Spencer prayed over the feast and over the family coming together to feast.

It is early morning and time to hit the road again. Tyrone announced, "It is too early for breakfast so we will start our morning with coffee poured in our mugs." Everyone agreed as they hugged and said their goodbyes. The kids were still asleep at 5:00 A.M. Before they took to the road the husbands made a confession to their wives.

Tyrone spoke up, "Lacy and I were unable to purchase tickets for the cruise to Hawaii because it was fully booked. However, we were able to book a cruise to Jamaica, and that's what we did." There was sudden dancing around and singing from both ladies, "Ja-mai-ca, Ja-mai-ca, I make love in Ja-mai-ca. They all laughed for a long time.

Sixteen

ON THE ROAD AGAIN
(Final Destination-Miami Florida)

....

'Well everybody, we're back on the road again, just the four of us." "Tyrone thanks for taking the wheel first. After everybody went to bed, I stayed up all night talking to my brother. It had been a long time since we saw each other and we had a lot to talk about. I can say that brother of mine is a happy man. He said that his wife is everything he could ever want in a woman. He's going to bring his whole family to visit with me and my family at the end of next school year. Samantha Skye will be out of our lives by then I hope, dead or alive, as long as she is gone. I am going to take a nap, wake me when you stop for breakfast, and ladies forgive me for going out on you like this. I am a tired sleepy man this morning."

Tyrone will get the quiet time he needs because nobody is talking or playing the radio. Two or three hours, is good to just relax and enjoy the ride. Once they get to Georgia, they're half way there. Their first stop since gassing up in Alabama is a small town outside Atlanta, Georgia where they will stop for a late morning breakfast. Soon they will be back on the road full of energy.

"Tyrone, I need just three more hours and I'll be ready to take the wheel." "Lacy, why don't I just keep it going until, we reach Florida. We will still have several hours to go before we reach the Gold Coast of Florida. I will turn the wheel over to you as soon as we cross over from Georgia to Florida or at the first stop for travelers." Imani spoke up, "We'll all have to be quiet for a little while longer so Lacy can get the rest he needs. All of us got a good night's sleep because we turned in early, but Lacy didn't because he wanted to spend as much time as possible with his brother and catch up on family news." "Monique spoke up, "Imani is right and we all need to relax as much as possible. Once we get to Miami and board that ship, I don't think any of us will be getting much rest. As I remember, there is so much to do that you can party all night long if you got the energy. For gamblers, the casino is popping 24/7. Of course that leaves us out since we are not gamblers." Tyrone spoke up quickly, "I don't know about you, but with me, I'm game and I plan is do a little bit of everything and I hope my wife is with me while I'm doing it all." "Don't worry, Tyrone, I'll be with you and if we're separated we'll still be connected by our cell phones. I'm going to keep up with my baby."

Finally, the travelers reached the Florida line and Tyrone decided to stop at a rest stop before gassing up for the road. Tyrone made a suggestion while at the rest stop and everyone agreed right away. "Finding a restaurant nearby and having an early dinner before we continue is a great suggestion Tyrone, I think I am speaking for everyone" "Thanks, everyone, ha, ha, ha." Imani added; we can then take the turnpike all the way into the Southern part of Florida and on to Miami." "Damn, we make a good traveling team." "Yes we do Tyrone, yes we do."

GOOD EATS AND BACK ON THE ROAD

....

After having dinner at a nice little southern diner, the travelers were back on the road again. "I am feeling good about this trip to Florida and the cruise to Jamaica. "Lacy, and you to Tyrone, don't forget that you two need to call your office and tell Cheryl that you will not be back to the office for the next couple of weeks. Maybe you should tell her that you are away on a much needed vacation to get much needed rest." "Lacy, my man, maybe when you talk to Cheryl about our court schedule, you should tell her to cancel all dates until further notice, and that she needs to call our clients and cancel all appointments, and let them know that she will call them to set up new appointments at a later date." "Tyrone, I will make the call from the ship first thing Monday morning, now let's forget about that woman for now." "Lacy, thank you, amen, amen, amen." "Monique, shut up, shut up, shut up." "Tyrone, stick it where it hurts."

"Tyrone, the song coming on the radio, I'm dedicating to you, "I'm So In Love With You," by Anthony Hamilton and Jill Scott." "Ha, ha, ha, ha, ha, ha, ha, I know this man is not trying to sing this song to Monique." "Imani, you're wrong, you're so wrong, ha, ha, ha, ha, ha." Who turned the radio off?" "I'm sorry Tyrone; you know it was all in fun, ha, ha, ha, ha."

"Everyone, get your change together we're about to get on the turnpike. Dump your change in the tray up front. It's going to be smooth riding all the way with no turns or getting off the highway, let's all just sit back and enjoy the long ride and think, "destination Miami and ultimate destination, Jamaica and surrounding Islands. Can anyone beat that?" Lacy yelled from the driver's seat, "Not even with a stick." Monique yelled out "let's sing a road song! Everybody yelled out in unity, "Tyrone, why don't you start with one of our sing-a-long oldie songs."

Before long, everybody was singing and having fun. They continued singing their favorite songs, one after another for about an hour. "Monique, I'm glad you suggested that Tyrone and Lacy ride up front and you and I take the back seat." "Imani, let's talk about the outfits we picked from your boutique for this trip. Do you think our husbands will let us wear our sexy swimwear on the beaches while we are on the Islands touring, I know it has to be at least one stop where we can go to the beach, what do you think about it." "Monique, I intend to wear my swimsuit even if it's at the pool on the ship. I plan to make a lot of females jealous, so it's the beach or one of the pools on the ship, or only in our rooms and that maybe the case and that is what I have to say about it." The men were eavesdropping, "what do you have to say about it, Lacy?" "I think our wives have made decisions about this trip where they didn't include us husbands. "What do you have to say about our wives doing such a thing, Lacy?" "I am going to let my wife give me the answer to that question. "Imani, start talking, I would like to hear your answer, hell, Tyrone and I both would like to know that answer." "Monique why are you so quiet, am I going to be the heavy in this?" "Imani tell my husband for me that I am so in love with him." Imani spoke with an exclamation sound in her voice tone, "subject closed, let's move on to something new." "Tyrone, I think we just got slapped in the face." Tyrone spoke with a smile on his face, "you think, huh?"

"Husbands and I speak for myself and for my friend here in the back seat with me, while we are on this cruise, you will be taken good care of by your wives, and you will most certainly get whatever, both your hearts desire." "To both wives in the back seat, and I'm speaking for both myself and Lacy, this is going to be a second honeymoon you will never forget, and never stop talking about." The ladies started giggling, and Monique leaned over and whispered in Imani's ear, "we got'um", and Imani whispered back, "in the palm of our hands." Tyrone turned the radio up and they all started singing. They passed through West Palm Beach, still bopping and singing, straight down the unending road headed south.

ENTERING THE CITY OF MIAMI

…………………………………………...

Lacy spoke first, "Finally, we're here, we, just entered the city of Miami." Tyrone spoke up, "Yes, and we have only two hours to find the dock where we will board the ship to Jamaica." "Imani, girl, we will be sleeping aboard the ship tonight and soon we'll be in paradise making love on the beach." You talk like you know some secret place on the beach to steal away in secrecy." There's one of those on most beaches you go to so why would Jamaica be different. I am going to dress sexy and have fun, fun, fun." "In that case our husbands will have their eyes on us every waking moment."

Tyrone made a quick announcement, "Listen everybody, I think we need to have our proper ID ready for traveling overseas. I know we will most likely stand in a long line to board the ship but we should not fumble around looking for anything." "Tyrone, I think what you are trying to say is that Imani and I should not have to search through our purses for needed documents such as our passports, right?" "Let's face it ladies, things can get lost in one of those purses I see you carrying." "Us ladies would like to carry your money in our purses." Everybody burst out in a big laugh. Everybody looked in amazement as they watched the big ship in their view.

"Ladies, I will let you out at the docks where everybody is taking their luggage and you can take care of ours while Lacy and I take care of parking our cars for this cruise, and remember to please have your papers handy for view, if or when needed."

ON THE SHIP AT LAST

....

"Lacy, our room is very spacious and it looks nice. I am going to enjoy a week in this room with you." "Imani, these walls will be holding a lot of secrets after we leave. If these walls could talk, Imani, you could get a book from this room." "Honey, let's go next door and see how our friends are doing." Not right now baby, I want to unpack first. Let's give them time to settle in first." "While you're unpacking our suitcases, I'll take a quick nap before I shower and dress for the evening." "Lacy, please don't plan for a long evening. I think we both should go to bed early tonight and get up early tomorrow morning, well rested, wide awake and with plenty energy. I want to enjoy all our stops on this cruise." "Imani, I can guarantee you that this will be an event we will be talking about when the two of us can do no more than sit side by side in our rocking chairs and talk about this cruise." "I am tired but I can't let my husband go out on the ship at night alone. There are just about as many hens on the prowl as there are roosters out there prowling around."

Lacy is up early and already dressed with a big appetite for breakfast. "Honey, I'm almost ready to go. Give me just thirty minutes and I'll be ready to join you for breakfast." "I'm counting the minutes, starting now." After thirty minutes waiting, Imani made her appearance and all Lacy could say is, "Damn, this is worth the wait. Imani, you are gorgeous, let's go get breakfast. Monique and Tyrone are waiting for us. I told them that you will be ready to go about this time."

Both couples decided to eat in the formal dining room instead of buffet style in the food courts. In about two hours the ship will make its first stop for touring. "Imani, it looks like our husbands can't take their eyes off their wives." "Monique, it is very noticeable, and Tyrone can't seem to stop drooling just being close to you. In a couple of hours we will leave the ship for a full day of fun just watching our husbands, watch us. Girl, get your camera ready." Imani, I hope our husbands have their charge cards ready for action because I plan to buy at least one expensive item at each touring stop. I'm looking at maybe a ring at one stop, a pair of earrings at another stop and in Jamaica, maybe a necklace and a bracelet. "The way they're slobbering over us we will get whatever we want and they are ready to give it to us. They love us and we love them." "Monique, I think you know that we are going to have to lead them to the jewelry stores, they will not automatically take us there." "Yes, I know, and I also know that their eyes will be following two asses they can't take their eyes off. We picked the right wardrobe for this trip." "Yes we did, and we don't have to worry about them wandering off or looking at other women while on this cruise." "Girlfriend, I am working it," and Monique smacked her own ass.

"Lacy, the Island is beautiful. You picked the perfect cruise for our honeymoon. If Jamaica is as beautiful as this island, I can't wait to get there." "Imani, the joy I see in your eyes tell me everything. It's the excitement of seeing the beauty of the island with you is what gives me pure joy." "Lacy, will you look at Monique and Tyrone. The two of them look so happy and in love, what could be more beautiful? Let's go join the beautiful couple and invite them to stroll with us. I saw a jewelry store while we were walking and I want to check it out. Is that okay with you, sweetheart?" "It's fine with me, I will let Monique and Tyrone know of our plan." Imani just smiled and as she turned to walk away, she gave a diva headshake.

After getting back on the ship, both couples went to their rooms and relaxed for a little while before getting ready for dinner and a little dancing at one of the clubs. "Lacy, since the evening is still early why don't we take the ladies to the comedy club." "That sounds good to me, my brother." "Husbands, as you already know, Imani and I are crazy about jazz, so is it asking too much if we can end the evening relaxing with a mild mixed drink at the jazz club?" "Monique, it is perfect what do you think, Lacy?" "Perfect."

It is early Tuesday morning and Imani does not know that the full day and evening has been planned for her. The two men and Monique had gotten together before the cruise and put together a plan for a small gathering. They counted on a few people who they met while on the ship to join them in the celebration.

"Imani, the honeymoon starts today." "What does that mean, Lacy?" "It means that this room will be seeing a lot of us today and this bed will feel a lot of us today. I will go out to the food courts and get our breakfast, and I will not forget your coffee. I will bring back a little of everything and we can share. I will first go and get the coffee and the toast and biscuits, butter, and the cream and sugar for your coffee. I can't bring back everything a one time. I'll be right back." "Thanks Lacy, I am ready for my coffee."

"Lacy, this breakfast is great. It is so relaxing sitting out here on the balcony of our room while eating and sipping coffee." "Imani, this is your day. I want to wait on you and take care of your needs. I think it is about time I do for you some of the things you have always done for me." Imani and Lacy lounged on the balcony for about an hour just staring at the wide open ocean and enjoying the calmness, and the warmth of the sun.

Rrrrring, rrrrring, rrrrring, "hello," "hello Imani, I missed you and Lacy at breakfast this morning. How, are things going on with you?" "Things are going very well with me. I'm on my second honeymoon, and I'm loving it." "Tyrone said that we're supposed to have lunch together. I'm looking forward to seeing you and all of us spending time together." Monique, I will be there looking my prettiest."

"Tyrone, Imani doesn't have a clue that a party has been set up for her. She doesn't know that one of my suitcases was filled with her books. It was a good idea for Lacy to order them and give our address for receiving the shipment. Tyrone, thanks for making room in one of your suitcases for my, clothing." "Remember Monique, everything have to be setup and ready for the party by 12:30, and Lacy will escort Imani in shortly thereafter." "It will be ready, I promise. I can hardly wait for this event to take place."

"Tyrone, we picked the perfect time for this celebration. Most of the people on the ship are stirring around and we picked a table in a nice corner with our backs to the wall. We can see everyone coming and going." "I see the balloons floating from the table center are the same as you two ladies sorority colors, and before you say a word, I don't see a thing wrong with it."

"Tyrone, there is something I want to say to you. Sweetheart, I want to thank you for making the change with our vacation destination. I personally think that we will have more fun in Jamaica than we would have had in Hawaii. I know Hawaii has the reputation for romance in paradise, but I never heard the word fun in the mix, and when Jamaica is mentioned it seems to have it all, especially the fun part of it, which is important. Imani liked the change also, and she has already thanked Lacy for the change. This is certainly a grand vacation so far." Thanks, baby."

A SURPRISE WITHIN A SURPRISE

....

Imani could not believe she had walked into a surprise party arranged for her. She thought that she was a part of arrangements for the celebration of her new book. "I can't believe you, my friends and my husband was able to keep this from me. How did you get a cake made with my book cover decorated on it?" "Imani, I was afraid that you would catch on when the two of us were not spending time together aboard the ship. We made the final arrangements when Lacy stopped by our room this morning on his way to get your breakfast. We wanted everything to be perfect for you." "Everybody this party is perfect, thank you."

"You're welcome, LET THE PARTY BEGIN! And don't forget to open your presents."

The Haywills joined the Balls in their room to finish the celebration. "Lacy, this diamond bracelet you gave me is beautiful. It is the same bracelet I tried on a couple months ago when Monique and I were out shopping for special scented candles and decided to stop at the jewelry store to look at some earrings. I saw this bracelet and tried it on but the price made me change my mind about it." "I told Lacy about it and we both agreed that it would make the perfect gift." Later they toured the ship.

By late evening, Imani got another surprise. "Is that my book I see the lady reading? Over there, I see a man with my book. Lacy, what is going on, is there something you have not told me yet?" "Sweetheart, I gave a few of your books away for publicity. We can't sell your books on the ship but I brought plenty to sell on the Island and there is contact in the books for feedback. Baby, I got a gut feeling that this book will put you on top with the #1 best sellers and I am so proud of you."

Back at the suite, "Monique, what's with the hand up?" "Tyrone, I think it would be in good taste to end this evening of celebration with drinks and a card game, but this time I want it to be ladies against the men." "Let's make a bet, ladies." "Lacy, since we're in your room, you be the honor of naming the bet." "Monique, I will make it easy for you ladies." "I bet you will ha ha ha ha"; "the losers will go to the food court, get the food and drinks and set the table for dinner here in this room." Imani spoke softly, "We need to come up with a plan on what we are going to do about Samantha Skye. We've got to make our families safe." Monique spoke up, "You're right about that one Imani. Why don't we move to the balcony after dinner so we can breathe, in fresh ocean air while discussing that skank."

"I have forgiven my husband for what I know had to be a mistake. Without a doubt it was a mistake, but the woman who is in our lives is like an infected sore and we must do something about it before it becomes a poison mass of puss in our lives. We know that Samantha Skye is mentally disturbed, and we also know that she is capable of doing just about anything to anyone, and I don't fall short of saying the word murder. We need to keep her fresh in our minds until she is long gone away from the metro area and us. I feel like going a step further and say, or dead"

Monique eyes brighten up and suddenly she said with a big smile on her face, "Tomorrow we will be in Jamaica." Tyrone stood up and announced, "There will be no mention of that woman on the Island of Jamaica, is that clear? "Yes" was said by everyone at the same time.

Seventeen

"Tyrone, we've been back home for two weeks now and no sight of Samantha. There is no sight or word concerning that woman and that is scary. It is just too damn quiet for me. I know she is up to something." "Monique, it is more like up to no good." "I talked with Ms. B and I told her that our original plan is still in effect and I told her that I want to have a meeting at my office once a week, just us three ladies." "Lacy and I will try to have lunch together as much as possible either at the office or at court." "Tyrone, the two of us make a great husband and wife team."

It's been two weeks since the trip and the kids are still talking about the fun they had. "Tyrone have you realized that the vacation we went on was the wise thing to do just as you had predicted. The kids are already planning for a next trip down there. They didn't even miss us." "They didn't have a chance to miss us Monique, they were having too much fun. 'As a matter of fact, I plan for the whole family to take the trip back down there when Lacy take his family. Of course, we will stay at a traveling lodge or a hotel. We don't want to crowd the farmhouse with lots of guests for a whole week. The kids can stay at the farm with everybody else and we will visit during the day. Imani and Lacy wouldn't mind looking after them during our absence." Before Monique could walk away, Tyrone reached out and pulled her close to him and looked into her eyes and humbly said to her, we will handle Samantha Skye and send her on her way.

NEVER UNDERESTIMATE A DEVIOUS WOMAN

....

Samantha has put away her sketches for her new designs. She must concentrate on her plans so that nothing can possibly go wrong. Because she is a city girl no one will ever believe that she would venture into unknown territory such as the wooded area of Michigan's Upper Peninsula or a nice house tucked away in the Jackson, Michigan area. Both places are in perfect locations for her purpose of living there, and tomorrow she will check to see if the houses are still up for sale. Either one of them will be the perfect place for her to set traps for intruders while she is in hiding after she has kidnapped the Ball twins. Meantime, her plan is to keep a place in the city for camouflage. She wants them to think that she is still in her condo in Detroit. After all she has leased it for a year, and it is paid up for six months. "One more week of going over my notes and doing a critical check against my visual-observation, and I will be ready to carry out my plan. My only wait I should have before I carry out my final plan is to have legal access to the house in the country."

She was told that it might take another week for the final papers to come through and the keys to the property will be turned over to her. Since Samantha is a patient woman, she can wait it out, and one week is not a long time to wait.

THE PLANNING OF SAFETY FROM SAMANTHA HAS FAILED

……………………………………………

As Imani and Monique sat in the Principal's office waiting for her to come speak with them, Imani started feeling a touch of fear as if something terrible was about to happen. It must have shown on her face because Monique asked her if something was wrong. Imani could no longer sit so she got up and begin to pace the floor and peeping out the door to the inner office where everybody was busy clearing things away for the day to go home. The principal suddenly appears with a smile on her face.

"Mrs. Ball, I was worried at first but I have been told that your daughters got a ride home from school with a family friend, who is also an employee here at our school. She is your friend, Samantha Skye." Imani stood in a frozen position, unable to speak. "Is there a problem Mrs. Ball"? Monique quickly spoke up, "she is not a friend to the Ball family. Samantha Skye is a threat to the Ball family. I think it is time for you to call the police and report a possible kidnapping at your school." Monique was already on her cell phone calling her husband, Tyrone. In about twenty minutes Tyrone showed up with Lacy, and the police arrived just about the same time.

Imani is beside herself and nobody is able to calm her down. Monique is trying hard to calm Imani but it is impossible. "I think it is time we called her doctor." "I don't need a doctor, I need my twin girls. Lacy, what have you done? Answer me damn-it, it is all your fault, I hate you". As Imani falls to her knees in a traumatized state, Lacy stands nearby watching her with tears streaming down his face. Imani falls closer to the ground looking toward the sky with tears flowing down her face. "Oh God, please help me. Please bring my girls home and safe in my arms. I am praying to you, Heavenly Father to please have mercy on me.

I need your embrace because I know that I can't make it without you. My heart is aching and I don't know what to do to ease the pain, please help me."

Imani feels like she has come to the end of the road with no way to turn except back which leads to another dead end for her. She is feeling that without her children there is no life for her. Imani also feels that the other woman and her husband, Lacy has destroyed their marriage. I wish the hell that he had just run off with the other woman with whom he feels that he would prefer being with rather than his wife and children. Samantha Skye is not to blame for all what is happening because Lacy played a lead role in it too. Right now, Samantha and Lacy is causing me so much grief until I just don't know how I'm going to make it from one day to the next. If anything should happen to my girls while they are in the hands of Samantha, I don't think it is possible for me to go on living, I don't think my heart could hold up under that kind of pressure. All I know to do and can do is put all my trust in the Lord and as of this moment, I give it all to my Heavenly Father, I now place it at the foot of the Cross.

(Meantime at a hideaway in Northern Michigan)
Early Evening

....

Samantha is thinking, "It was a good idea to have a restaurant type freezer installed here in my home. I have enough food stored to last a long time. I would say that maybe I have enough meats, vegetables, and sorted can foods to last about a year or longer. I have enough flour, corn meal, sugar, canned milk as well as powder milk to feed a troop of soldiers in training at Camp somewhere up there in Battle Creek, Michigan."

"Stacey and Lacey, I am still trying to reach your mom and dad on their cell phones numbers you gave to me. They are not answering either one of them and it sounds like they're having trouble on their lines. You know, it may be that they are at an out of area location for their phone service and we can't make connection. Any way it goes, they know that you girls are safe with me and, after all I am a family friend and also an employee at your school. I don't understand why they have you in that high class, state of the art school that looks down on the poor and the middle class folks who are working hard, just trying to keep their heads above water and give their children a good education, too. Girls, I need help in the kitchen, so please feel free to help me. I have already told you that my home is your home too, and I want you girls to feel comfortable in our home."

Samantha does not know what her next plan will be, but she does know that she will have to come up with something that is believable because the Ball twins are not stupid girls. Samantha knows that a plan has to be put in place within the next twenty four hours.

DAY TWO OF THE KIDNAPPING
7:30 A.M.

....

Imani has been given a strong medication to calm her down and to help her to get the much needed sleep she needs. Even with the medication that was prescribed for her seems not to work very well. Her eyes seem to carry a permanent shade of red.

Imani pushes herself up from her bed, and with swollen dark circled eyes, she stumbles down the hall and slowly walks down the stairs pausing slightly at each stair. When Lacy turned around and saw her standing there in the doorway of the kitchen wearing only the gown she had slept in, he quickly took off his robe and put it around her as he smiled and gave her a loving kiss on her cheek. "Good morning sweetheart. Sweetheart, I am preparing breakfast for us and I have coffee perked just the way you like it. Why don't you sit while I pour you a cup of your favorite coffee." Imani seems to be in a zombie like state, and with very little focus she walks to the table and sits without saying a word, not even a good morning or thank you. Lacy poured Imani a cup of coffee and also a cup for himself. Lacy did not try to talk to Imani because he already knows that she wants to know only about the twins. He also knows that Imani's zombie appearance is due to the effect of the depressant drug that the doctor has her taking.

Lacy is afraid to leave his wife at home alone because of her state of mind. He does not want her to cause harm to herself. Lacy also knows that he cannot bear to lose his whole family. "Without Imani, I will not want to live because I know now that her life and my life, is as one and can be separated only by God. What man separates is the body but no man can touch the spirit, so the two of us will eternally be connected."

Lacy always knew that he loved his wife Imani, but he didn't know how deeply and emotionally he needed her love and support until the tragedy that has plagued their lives and is now taking a toll on them. Right now Imani is blaming him and he is blaming himself. Lacy believes that he allowed Satan to come in and as always, it was lust that was used as a weapon against his better judgment. He now realizes what looks good to the eyes and feels good to the body is the temptation that is hard to resist for some men, especially if they are not in the word; of course Lacy is learning to pray and have personal talks with God. It is something he learned from Imani.

"I wish that I could take all that I have done back and erase it to a state of obliteration. I never felt so guilty about something in all my life. Also, I never thought that I would hate another human being as much as I hate that Samantha Skye. For the first time in my life I realize the possibility that I could kill another person, and right now I could kill

Samantha Skye". As Lacy gets deeper in his thoughts of what is happening to his family, he goes even deeper into his plans to commit murder. Every time he sees the agony on the face of his dear sweet innocent wife, he wants to scream out from the pain within himself. For the first time, with tears forming in his eyes, Lacy actually falls to his knees, and with both hands stretched toward the sky he commence to pray, "Dear God in Heaven, if you give my family back to me I promise you with all my heart that I will be a good righteous husband and father for my family. I will fellowship each week with other Christians and I will be at my wife's side as we enter the house of the Lord. I will keep my promise to you Heavenly Father, my God Almighty and this I pray to you, in Your Son Jesus name, Amen."

MID MORNING AT BROWN SUGAR'S
BEAUTY SHOP
10:00 A.M.

....

"Ladies, and you too Luscious, Monique paid me a visit early this morning with bad news about someone we all know and care about. She said that the Ball twins have been kidnapped from their school by Lacy's lady friend, Samantha Skye. I know you girls and you too Luscious, remember Samantha. The last time I saw that freaky bitch was the day I threw her scheming black ass out through that door of this beauty shop. Listen up ladies and you too, Luscious, we must get our old posse together, they're brothers who don't mind breaking bones, if that's what it comes to while handling business. The only important thing for us right now is to find the Ball twins and take care of that no good down in the gutter snake in the grass Samantha Skye. When the boys get here we must come up with a good plan for rescuing the twins without causing harm to them. I will call Imani and let her know that we will be doing all that we can do to help bring the twins home safe." Monique told Ms. B that a private detective who is often used by the Haywill/Ball Law Firm is already on the case. She thanked Ms. B for her help also.

AN ISOLATED COMMUNITY OUTSIDE JACKSON, MICHIGAN

....

Buzz, buzz, buzz, buzz, buzz ------It's 6:30 a.m., who in hell would be calling on someone this early in the morning, and the devil in Hell knows that this is the wrong house to be calling on." As Samantha's crazy thoughts continued to run wild with her as she rushed to the front door to answer it and to see who is laying on her doorbell and to put a stop to it before it wakes the twins. "Good morning, may I help you sir?" The man at the door hesitated for a moment, I am not sure if I am at the right place. Is this the Mark resident, Florida and Ray Mark?" "No, this is not the Mark resident, and

I don't recognize the name as one I know or even heard of." Clearing his throat and paying close attention to Samantha's face and eyes expression, he said to her, "uh, uh Ms., Mrs. Uh, uh, what did you say your name is?" "I did not say and neither did you". "I'm sorry about that ma'me, my name is Virg Lanne. May I use your phone, please?" "And where is your cell phone, if you don't mind me asking?" "I must have left it somewhere, I just don't know where. I will pay you for the use of your phone, and I promise you it will only take a moment." "I have a phone in my den near the entrance that you may use if you will walk straight ahead and turn left at the first opening, the phone jack is on the right hand side, and if the phone is not on the hook, look on the table to your left."

Samantha is not a stupid woman and she felt that extra sense of perception that warns her when danger is near. And just as she had figured it to happen, Mr. Virg Lanne walked from the den and started into another part of Samantha's house. "Where are you going, the front entrance to outside is this way." "I'm sorry Ms. Skye, I made a wrong turn." Mr. Lanne walked quickly toward the front entrance when Samantha stopped him. "Mr. Lanne, I have not had breakfast yet and I was about to have coffee and toast with cooked apples, why don't you join me in the kitchen." "I would like very much to join you Ms. Skye, I too have not had breakfast yet." "I was thinking Mr. Lanne, since it is such a nice day why don't we take our breakfast out to the patio and sit near the pool. It is really a beautiful day." The farm area is so beautiful this time of year in Michigan just before winter sets in. The change of leaves with their fall colors are breathtaking. "Ms. Skye, you have a beautiful home, and this is such a beautiful area to enjoy your beautiful home. The countryside is always beautiful to me, although I'm a city-man myself. I was born and raised in the city." "What part of the city do you live Mr. Lanne?" Before you answer that, I think it would be in good taste for me to call you Virg and you call me Samantha since we arc sitting here engaging in casual conversation." "I agree with you Samantha and thank you for making me feel welcome in your home." "I never thought that I would ever hear myself saying this but, it really is a pleasure having you here for breakfast. I don't usually get early morning company because I live so far away from everything." "Does that mean there is no Mr. Skye?" "Not anymore. We went our separate ways three years ago and I ended up here in this place with my two daughters. They may be coming down for breakfast soon and will they be surprised to see company all the way out here so early in the morning." As Samantha speaks, she is also thinking about how she will get rid of this man before the twins see him. "By the way Virg, what community do you live in?" "I live just outside the city of Detroit in Southfield, Michigan. Do you ever come to the city of Detroit, Samantha? With three casinos, the big Motor City gets a great number of visitors from across the state daily. The casinos are packed 24/7 continuously throughout the year." "Very seldom do I get to the city, but Virg, I would like to have lunch or dinner with you sometime soon. If you would like, we could meet halfway between where I live and where you live. I would like to drive into the city for lunch, how about it Virg?" "Samantha, all you have to do is call me and it's a date." Samantha is thinking, "to mess with me is like putting a gun to your head and pulling the trigger. Nobody, and I mean nobody mess with Samantha Skye and live a peaceful life. I will find out what he is up to if I have to kill him in the process. I can and I will be my enemy's worst nightmare, just don't piss me off."

12th PRECINCT
8:30 A.M.
DAY 5 OF THE KIDNAPPING

……………………………………

"Good morning, Mr. & Mrs. Ball. I am glad you both were able to come in to see us this morning. Detective Troyer will be with you shortly. I will let her know that you have arrived." "Thank you, sir." Detective Troyer's assistant, Mr. Charles walks in at that moment.

"Good morning, Mr. and Mrs. Ball. I am Detective Troyer's assistant, Mr. Charles. Will you please come with me to the conference room. I have coffee and donuts set and you are welcome to it. As a matter of fact, I think I will have coffee and donut with you. I hope you like regular coffee because we ran out of the decaf. I also have a setup for tea lovers, hot water and lemon slices." "This is very kind of you and Detective Troyer, thank you for making us feel comfortable." "You are truly welcome, and also this will give me a chance to talk with you and see how things are going so for, and you already know that I will be working with Detective Troyer on your case." "Do you know how long it will be before Detective Troyer will be joining us?" "It shouldn't be much longer unless she ran into a problem. She is heading an important conference call that is connected to other offices across the state of Michigan. This telephone conference will determine and off-set the annual conference that is held annually somewhere in the state. I'm sure this is of no interest to you. It is something that would be of interest only to a politician. Mr. and Mrs. Ball, while we were waiting, why don't you tell me all that you know about Samantha Skye and I will take notes for Detective Troyer and have them quickly typed for her meeting with you this morning. Of course you will be asked by her to go over some things again during your conversation with her." "Mr. Charles, we are willing to do everything that we can to help bring our girls back home to us." "Let's start with your twin girls' name, age and description."

SAMANTHA'S MASTERPIECE AT WORK

....

Samantha hears talking coming from the twins bedroom. She knows that she has to have answers for them before they start asking questions, and it has to be something they want to hear. "Stacey and Lacey, are you out of bed yet? I have a great breakfast for you girls this morning. I also have good news about an early morning visitor I had this morning who proved to be of help to us about Hurricane Katrina in New Orleans. As soon as you have dressed and had breakfast we will talk," As Samantha hurriedly started preparing for breakfast for the second time, her thoughts pondered on what she could do to cover her tracks with information to the twins. Having cable has kept them from watching the news, and I have also turned my head when I know damn well that they are in their room watching an adult channel because I have heard the lustful lovemaking sounds as I passed the door to their room. Samantha must do whatever it takes to prolong the time it takes to do what she has to do., short of killing the twins which is something she may have to do anyway. At this point and time, if pushed it may take place anyway.

As Virg Lanne heads toward I-94, he is in deep thought. "I wonder if Samantha caught on that I didn't just happen to be in her area and got lost. I have been offered big bucks to find her and the Ball twin girls. For me, it is strictly business, and if Samantha can beat the offer that has been given me by a few thousand, I will turn and walk away and never look back. I will allow her to offer a payoff once I am certain that the Ball girls are safe from harm. Samantha is a beautiful sexy woman, which makes it easy to date her. I also know that she is a dangerous woman and not to take her for granted because the wrong move with her may be my last move. Knowing this, I still feel a strong sexual drive toward her. She is a beautiful young woman and could have easily gotten herself a sugar daddy. Something tells me that Samantha is a little too high maintenance for the average sugar daddy. She is not the one to live in the ghetto while sugar daddy's love ones live a different lifestyle reaping a better side of life with a real God given future. It's a

shame she couldn't find a man who was right for her. I am too young to be her old fool, but I would love to spend a little between-the-sheet time with her. As it stands, being a man, I'm going to damn try. I think I will plan to meet with her very soon, but right now, business is business."

"Girls, why don't we set up for breakfast out on the patio. It is such a pleasant day to sit out and talk while enjoying this grand weather. I want us to take as long as we need since there is no place I need to be anytime soon. Talk to me, girls, tell me what is on your mind". As Stacey and Lacey busy themselves setting up and transporting food from the kitchen to the patio, they began talking about how they missed their mom and dad. "Girls we can talk as soon as we are seated for breakfast. It is important that we say our grace first. We must give thanks to the Lord for all that we receive." Samantha is thinking how she almost believes what she is saying. "I think this is about the time when you say lightning will come down and strike my black ass." "What did you say Ms. Samantha"? "I thought I heard lightening strike and hope the storm will pass. It's nothing Stacey, nothing at all. Girls, I was thinking earlier about something our visitor said this morning. I'm sorry you missed the chance to meet him. I will tell you girls everything he told me. By-the-way, His name is Virg Lanne, he is about thirty five years old, he is single and he lives in Southfield, Michigan. I told him that I may be calling on him.

Eighteen

THE POSSE GATHERS AT BROWN SUGAR'S BEAUTY SHOP

....

Gunsta Pete was the first to arrive at the shop. The shop crew was glad to see him and right away the ladies and Luscious too, wanted to know what's been happening with him since they last saw him which has been a few months. Gunsta Pete's response to them was, "just keeping the cutie pies happy, and believe me, there are plenty of them around." As always, Gunsta Pete is dressed sharp and looking good. It has to be nice to the eyes to scan the full body view of a fine brother. Mmmmm, the brother is six feet tall sporting a body that shows he works out regularly, mmmmm. It's only for the single women. All others carry a claim ticket/paper legal with two names attached.

Soon after Gunsta Pete arrived at the Beauty Shop, Ms. B's main posse crew member, big bad Mojo, Mr. Marvin himself, also known as, Big Mo arrived. Ms. B right away closed up shop to have an emergency meeting. All parties had input in the planning for what needs to be done in rescuing the Ball twins. The one thing they all agreed on that must be done is to put some of the homeys out in the field where she has to and will surface if she is still in the area. There are three places we can almost count on for Samantha to go to and that is the drug store, the bank and the grocery store. All our street homeys will be given a photo of Samantha, showing a clear face shot and a full body shot of her. They will be like hound dogs on her trail. If anybody can sniff her out they can and will.

THE HAYWILL MANSION
MONDAY, EARLY MORNING

....

"Monique, I called Virg Lanne this morning and spoke with him about the progress report he is working on concerning Samantha. He wants to come over Wednesday morning and he sounded as if he may have good news for us. I told him that 9:00 a.m. would be a good time for him to come. I thought that maybe we can have breakfast set up for him and make him feel comfortable as possible as he delivers his report on the progress of what I will call, The Samantha Skye Case. Tell me if you think that I need to call him and make changes. I know how anxious you are to meet with him." "Thank you, sweetheart for acting so quickly for me. I feel like this is going to be a good meeting and you are right, we should have a grand breakfast for him on Wednesday morning. I can tell you now Tyrone, I will be busy in the kitchen, and if I need your help, I will call you." "Baby, I am so sorry that I have not been of any help to you lately. Since Lacy turned all his clients over to me, I have been busy day and night, and it's getting rough now that I am coming up for trials throughout the next few months. With my clients and Lacy's clients, my plate overflowing, and I don't know how much longer I can handle the overflow. I know that I have neglected you with things to do around the house and even our bedroom, and I really miss that action." "Don't worry about that, Tyrone." Monique paused for a moment. "With all the things that have been on my mind and the worrying I am still going through, my performance would be at a minimum standard, which is no more than a sexual release orgasm to help me sleep at night, if not the whole night."

"Monique, you are a very understanding wife. I can't relax because I have a lot of work to do. I have two court cases to prepare. I also have two clients to call and cancel their appointments for the upcoming week. I don't know how much longer I will be able to keep up with such a load of cases as I am now faced with." "Remember, you are doing it for your best friend who desperately needs you right now. Just let me know when you're ready for dinner, I prepared your favorite dish." "Again, thank you baby, for being so understanding and putting up with me."

GRAND BREAKFAST FOR VIRG LANNE

……………………………………………………

Virg was surprised to see such a big spread laid out for breakfast. First it was prayer and then the eating was on. Virg must have eaten some of everything on the table, from bacon, sausage, ham, steak, salmon fried with corn meal breading, along with grits, hash browns, pancakes/whole cakes, oatmeal, Texas style cheese toast, donuts, two kinds of egg omelets, scrambled eggs and several flavors of cream cheese, fruit spreads, a bowl of mixed chopped fresh fruit, whole fresh fruit, plenty to drink including to my surprise, a bottle of sweet wine.

"Well Mr. and Mrs. Haywill, this has been a grand breakfast and I must say you have made me feel special. Right now, I feel like a stuffed pig. Everything looked so good and tasted very, very, very delicious. You sure know how to spoil a person. Are you ready to hear some good news?" "Am I ready? Man you have just made my day, and I hope that I am speaking for Tyrone too." Tyrone spoke up very quickly. "Why don't we go to my office and talk." Virg followed Tyrone to his office and Monique followed behind after Virg. After Virg Lanne took a seat, he opened his brief case and handed a written report to Tyrone. Monique and Virg sat quietly while Tyrone went over the report. Looking up with a smile on his face, before he could say a word Monique jumped straight up out the chair, anxiously waiting to hear what Tyrone has to say even if she already knew it was all good. "Baby, please sit down, and let Virg do the talking." "Mr. and Mrs. Haywill, as you can see, I delivered a good report for you. My next step is to snatch the twins before Samantha catches on to me. I have developed a relationship with her and I am hoping that she goes after my bait. I plan to call on her for a date and if things work out as I expect it to, I will have the twins back home with their parents where they belong. Once I have gotten the twins out of Samantha's reach I will go after her criminal behind and turn her over to the police. Pray for me that I come out of this in one piece."

This has been a big day with everybody learning good things that seem helpful about Samantha. That is everybody, except Brown Sugar and her Posse. They are strictly out for blood, so it's a piece of Samantha's ass or nothing. Virg is the only one with a handle on what is happening and he is about to take it to the head.

Rrrrring, Rrrrring, Rrrrring, Rrrrring, "hold your horses, I'm coming, I'm coming, and this has better be important." "Hello, Samantha, I'm so sorry I disturbed you." Samantha quickly snapped into a friendly disposition. "Hello Virg, how are you? I was not expecting to hear from you so soon, where are you?" "I am at home right now, but I was wondering if you care to have an early dinner with me this evening? I will understand if you say no, after all, I did call you at the last minute?" "Stop it Virg, you know I will have dinner with you, what time will you pick me up?" Samantha, if it will not be too much a bother, would you mind meeting me at a restaurant here in Southfield, I will give you the address and directions, it will be easy to find." "Yes, I will meet you, give me a moment to get pen and paper and also the time you want me be there." She jumped into her car and headed down the highway and did not stop until she reached the home of the family where she left the twins. Virg was still waiting in secrecy nearby for Samantha to come home. She soon arrived home with the twins, and as Virg waited for them to go to bed and all lights off, to his surprise Samantha was leaving the house and this time she left the twins at home alone. Virg decided to follow her and see what she is up too. While he was in pursue of Samantha, he made a call on his cell phone to Monique and Tyrone to let them know where the twins are being kept and to get someone there in a hurry before Samantha returns home.

Virg followed Samantha back to I-94 but this time she was headed East which meant she was going to meet him as planned at the restaurant in Southfield. So far things are looking good for Virg and hopefully all goes well with his plan to rescue the twin girls. For Samantha to catch on could mean someone's death. She is bad to the bone.

VIRG LANNE'S ACTION PLAN AT WORK

....

Virg is thinking about the danger of what he is doing and the possibility of Samantha catching on to what he is doing and killing him. His plan is to get her away from the house long enough for him to get the twins out and away from that area as soon as possible and back in the arms of their parents. "I will park on one of the side streets and watch for her to arrive at the restaurant. I'm glad I thought to tell her that if I am not there when she arrives, she is to wait because I will be on my way. I told the front host at the restaurant Samantha's full name and to treat her like a celebrity visiting their establishment". Virg has already notified Tyrone and Monique, but what he didn't know was that Monique had notified Brown Sugar who shared the information with her posse.

Like clockwork, Samantha arrives on time. Meantime, Virg has doubled back and is already headed for her place in the woods. To his surprise, the house was empty, nobody at home, no sign of life. His guess is that she had someone to pick the girls up. She had become acquainted with a family close by in the area. The family has five children, all close in age and they have a daughter the same age as the twins. It was the perfect place to leave them for a few hours. Virg is really out done over the situation on hand. He is thinking, where the hell are the Ball twins? His next thought was to call Detroit and let someone know his dilemma. He made one call that quickly made a way to Ms. B's shop. Since Virg is one who does not give up so easy, he decided to hide out and wait for Samantha to return home.

Samantha was enjoying the special treatment given her, and it made her feel like a Very Important Person (V.I.P.). After about an hour she realized something was wrong and it didn't take her long to figure it out. Samantha suddenly became very angry and without a doubt, very clear in her mind, Virg's intent. She snapped up from her table and bolted from the restaurant like a shot of lightning. She did not stop until she reached her home where she left the twins.

The girls were fast asleep from a long busy day. Virg realized that the twins were at home and had gone to bed early when one of them walked across the room into the light. Suddenly to his surprise, Samantha came out the house and got into her car and very quickly sped off down the highway headed toward I-94. As Virg was in pursue of her, he made a call on his cell phone to Tyrone and Monique and told them where to find the twins and the urgency of time with the rescue.

Samantha changed over to the Southfield Freeway with full speed and didn't stop until she reached Macy's parking lot at Northland Shopping Center. She was not in there very long before she came out with two large pieces of luggage and put them in her SUV. Samantha made a call from her cell phone to Virg's cell phone, but no answer and this confirmed what she was thinking. She knows that dirty business is in progress and that she is the target. The woman is smart enough to know that someone has to be watching her so she must keep a look out and trick that person into view. All I can say is Lord have mercy on them because I the hell will not. Virg followed her down Greenfield Road to Outback Steakhouse Restaurant where she stopped to eat because she didn't get to eat at the restaurant where she went to meet with Virg. She didn't know it but he had paid for her dinner in advance at the other restaurant. Virg told them to put it on his tab so the restaurant was not at a lost. As Samantha waited for her dinner at the Outback, she made a phone call but Virg didn't know to whom it was made. The luggage obvious means she is taking a trip somewhere. Virg is thinking half talking to himself, "I've got to find out where she's going so somehow I will steal that phone from her." Virg suddenly had a look of disbelief on his face as he watched her from where he had been hiding out of sight.

Samantha got up from her seat and went to the lady's room and left her cell phone on the table. It took Virg less than one minute to swipe the phone from the table and was gone before Samantha returned to her table. He sat in his car and called the last number she called on her cell phone. The call was to a travel agency for a cruise. She was able to book a cruise at the last minute. Virg inquired about the cruise and they told him there

was one more cabin available but it was a large suite that will accommodate four people.

Virg booked the cabin and told the agent he would call back with the names. Since he is still on the case he will bill Attorney Tyrone Haywill. He gave the phone to someone who was going into restaurant and told them to give it to someone in charge and that he had picked it up from the floor and thought it was his phone, and that maybe the owner is still there. Virg had one more important call to make before calling it a night. Rrrrrring, rrrrrring, rrrrrring, rrrrrring, "Hello, the Haywills, Mrs. Haywill speaking, how may I help you?" "Mrs. Haywill, this is Virg Lanne, I am calling with good news, may I speak with your husband please." Monique took the phone to Tyrone immediately and stood by for the good news. Virg had also seen on her phone where she had called the airport, which meant she would be on her way to Miami for the cruise tomorrow.

"Monique, our prayers have been answered. The twins will soon be in our hands and out of the clutches of the wicked witch of hell bound. I will tell you all about it but first we must hurry to Lacy and Imani's house, we can talk in the car. Get on your cell phone and let them know we are on our way over and that I will explain everything when we get there." By the time they arrived at the Ball's place Tyrone had explained everything to Monique. Monique agreed with her husband that she should stay with Imani while the two men handle the job of rescuing the twins.

Heading down the highway the men talked about the strategy they will use for precaution. It is dust dark and the street lights are on. "Lacy, we will drive up like regular visitors and ring the front doorbell, and then wait to see what happens. This rescue is too easy and I feel uneasy about everything, what do you think about it? "Tyrone, I don't think Samantha will leave things wide open this way, she is too smart to let her guard down like that. We will have to play this one by ear. The house looks dark but I thought I saw a light on in one of the second floor rooms. I think we should ring the door bell anyway." After laying on the doorbell for about a minute, Lacy and Tyrone decided to leave and figure out some other way of getting to the girls and they needed to go back to the car and put their heads together and throw some ideas at each other for a tryout.

By the time the two men reached their car and before they entered there was a loud scream and before they could turn around all the way they heard someone yell out "daddy! Daddy"! By the time they had turned around Lacy was looking his girls in the face. He was so overcome with joy he began to cry. This time it was tears of joy.

Stacey spoke first, “Daddy, we were told not to answer the door for anyone not even the people we know. Ms. Samantha told us that even the people we know may present a danger to us. We heard about how some people have been trying to kill you. Lacey and I understand why we couldn’t see you and mama and Ms. Samantha had to keep us safe.
We thought at first you and mama was in New Orleans helping out the victims in the Katrina Hurricane.” “Lacey honey, are you alright, you’re so quiet.” “Yes daddy, now that you are here everything is alright.” “Girls, your mom and your god-mom are at the house waiting for us to bring you home safe. We will talk with you girls later about all that has taken place that you were not aware of. I thank God that you are safe and unharmed. Don’t bother to take anything from the house just get in the car and hurry, we must get going.” “What about Ms. Samantha Daddy?” “Don’t worry your pretty little head about Ms. Samantha, Stacey. She will get the reward due her and in due time.”

Samantha is now leaving the Outback Steakhouse Restaurant on Greenfield Road in Southfield, Michigan and the look she is wearing is not a relaxed look. As a matter of fact, she looks a little tense. “I have been calling the house and nobody is answering. What the hell is the matter? I know something is wrong. If the girls are not there, then somebody has taken them away. I have let Virg put me in a trick bag. While he was leading me away from the house, he must have doubled back and took the girls away from the house. I will settle my score with him at a later date, and it will most certainly happen. There is no reason for me to go home now, and worse of all, the police squad could be there to arrest me on the spot. The joke will be on them when I don't show up. I will shop for whatever I need when I need it. My present plan is to get to Florida and on that ship far away from here as I could possibly get." Samantha decided to call home again just in case the girls are still there. After several tries Samantha still was not quite satisfied, so she called her neighbor who had previously watched the girls for her. She told her neighbor that she had not been able to reach the girls by phone and if she would go to her house and check on them and let them know that she has been trying to reach them. Samantha soon got a call back and she was told that her house was empty, that there was no one there. She quickly came up with a lie that a family member had picked them up and that she had forgotten. There was no need to go back home since she always carry her important papers with her. Samantha put her foot on the gas leaving the Outback, headed South toward 8 Mile Rd. All on her mind at the moment was to get to the Southfield Freeway and on to I-94 and straight to the airport. Her plan is to stay overnight and catch an early flight out early in the morning. She doesn't have to be at the dock to board the ship until 4:00 P.M. tomorrow evening so that will give her plenty of time to rent a car at the airport and drive to her next destination while doing a little sight-seeing in Southern Florida.

"Oh my gosh!" "I'll be damned, my #1 enemy, Virg Lanne. I knew someone had to be close by keeping a watch on me. He is moving over to go into the opposite direction on Oak Park, Michigan side of Greenfield Road. He will not get away from me, he is a dead ass. I don't like being pissed off and now Virg to me is like a walking dead man waiting to see his maker." As Virg heads in the opposite direction toward I-696 Freeway, Samantha follows in pursuit with hurting him in mind. "If I don't kill him, he will wish he was dead. Just let him get on that freeway, I will have his car bouncing off the wall." As Virg makes a right turn onto the freeway entering Oak Park City Limit heading East Samantha yelled out, "That fool got on the freeway. He is asking for an accident, he will not get away from me. Virg picked up speed and so did Samantha. As she gained on him, he sped even faster but she kept getting closer and closer. He made a quick decision and got off at the exit of Dequindre in Warren, Michigan and headed toward Eight Mile Road full speed ahead hoping that he would get stopped by the police in the city of Warren but, no luck. When he got to Eight Mile, he made a right still speeding west down Eight Mile Road in the hopes of making it to I-75 or the Lodge Freeway. He crosses over I-75 full speed ahead. When he got to Greenfield Road he made a left turn into Detroit on Greenfield Road, headed to the freeway. He sped wide open on the Lodge and still no police car in sight. He finally got to the exit to lead him downtown where he knew there would be plenty law enforcement around for his safety from this crazy mad-woman. Virg was driving in so much fear that he didn't see Samantha exit at I-94 headed toward the Metro Airport in Taylor, Michigan.

IMPORTANT MEETING WITH THE POSSE

....

Virg meets with Ms. B, Big Mo, Gunsta Pete and Gunsta Pete's lady friend, Tiffany. Virg called Tyrone and told him to meet him at Ms. B's Beauty Shop. While waiting for Tyrone to get there, everybody is celebrating Virg as a hero and giving him his props for a job well done on leading the way in getting the Ball twins to safety. Ms. B blurts out, "Virg, I'm gonna make you one of my dogs yet."

Tyrone finally arrives at Brown Sugar Beauty Shop. "Good evening Mr. Haywill, I am very happy to see you. Hell, we are all very happy to see you. Mr. Lanne is here to talk to us all about something that is important. I'm sure it has something to do with that Samantha Skye". Tyrone greeted everyone and thanked them for giving the Ball family their support during such a rough time in their lives. Ms. B, you will always have a special place in my heart because of all you have done to protect and to show that you truly care about your friend Imani. I want you to know that you are welcome in my home anytime you want to visit my family, and you certainly will be on our guest list for social events. Please don't call me Mr. Haywill anymore, now that we are friends. To you and everybody else in this room, I am Tyrone, your new found friend".

"Virg, my man, now that we're all sitting, you got the floor." All attention is now on Virg Lanne, as he begins to speak. "You already know that I have been hired by Tyrone Haywill to hunt down Samantha Skye, the kidnapper of the twin daughters of Lacy and Imani Ball. I am here to give you updates on where I am with my quest at this time. It has not been easy, and as you know, I have been dealing with a dangerous woman. I can tell you as of now that the Ball twins are safe at home with their parents. I set up a scam for Samantha and she fell right into it. I was unsure at first that she would fall for it, and of course I had to move very quickly with my actions to rescue the twins. None of it could have been carried out without the help of their father, Lacy and your dear friend who is here with us now, our own Mr. Tyrone Haywill. I was tailing Samantha in her rental car and lost her just a little while ago when I called Tyrone and the two of us came up with the idea that Ms. B and her posse may be able to help with bringing the kidnapper to justice.

During my investigation, I discovered Samantha had booked a cruise and it is leaving out from Miami Beach, Florida tomorrow evening at 4:00 P.M. and that is why I am here now. I booked a cruise for four and it was the last one left. I also booked a flight for four out from Detroit Metro at 5:A.M. early morning. Ms. B, you will have to call to give the names of the people who will be going on this trip, I have the ticket information. We can all thank Tyrone for this sudden vacation. After the reservations arc in order we will discuss Ms. Samantha. It is important to know who you are dealing with. That woman doesn't stay long enough in one place for me to pinpoint her where about for me to call the police. The only time she was in one place was when she was with the twins and I could not gamble with the lives of those girls when they were in the hands of that crazy woman. The one thing I do know is that we cannot let her leave and disappear. She needs to pay for what she did, and she will have to be in the jurisdiction of the laws of the United States. Remember that all your contacts will be directly with Tyrone Haywill. Good luck and remember to be safe."

The posse arrives in Miami Beach, Florida. The posse numbered in three, Ms. B, Big Mo and Gunsta Pete. The fourth person on the trip is Gunsta Pete's lady friend, Tiffany, who Ms. B enjoys insulting and calls her Ms. Thang. It is 9:00 a.m. with a full day ahead of them before boarding the cruise ship. As always, Ms. B leads the way, but this time she hands the lead over to Big Mo with which he wears well. "Listen up posse, I think the first thing we need to do is rent a car. We should not spend the day here in Miami because we cannot take a chance on running into that devil witch. We can't afford to blow our cover. I know people in Liberty City and Richmond Heights and I also know a couple of folks over there at Florida Memorial

University, but all those places are too damn close. I think a good place to go is Fort Lauderdale, my old stomping grounds, but first I want to jump up there to Delray Beach and say hello to some folks and come on back down to Lauderdale and spend the rest of the day at an area I remember from my last visit. There is a large outdoor flea market that would take two or more hours to go through and there are great low prices on the merchandise. Let's all be watchful of the time, we don't want to miss the ship. I can holler at some home folks when we get back this way before we fly back to the Big D."

Nineteen

BOARDING THE SHIP

....

It is three o'clock by the time they returned the rental car back at the airport, and that gives them one hour to get to the dock to begin to start

boarding the ship. It also saves them money by taking the car back where they got it from.
The shuttle bus will take about 30 minutes to reach the dock which gives them plenty time to get themselves together for all that is needed once they're on the ship.

So far everything is running smoothly as they stand in a long line awaiting their turn to step forward and get their pictures taken which show-tell their beginning of fun, fun, fun on the big wide ocean. While standing in line, like the snap of the fingers, Ms. B took charge again. "Posse, listen up, this is very important. I think that maybe we ought to hang back at the tail end of the line because we don't know where in line Samantha is standing at this time. She knows who I am but she doesn't know who you two guys are, or what's-huh-name, Ms. Thang. I'm the one who has to be careful."

"Why don't we check to make sure our passports and credit cards are where we can get to them quickly." "Why do we need a credit card?" "Ms. Thang, the credit card is for the purpose of paying a percentage up front for room service and also to put money on your room key card to be used like a credit card while you are on this ship. No money is spent on the ship, you must use your room key card and if you should use it all, you can have more money put on it. All you don't use will be put back on your card at the end of the trip. You will need cash money and your regular credit card while we are on the Islands sightseeing if you want to purchase something. Ms. Thang, you're going to be with Gunsta Pete and he knows what to do. I know this is not his first cruise."

SAFELY IN THEIR SUITE

....

"Look at us in the beautiful top of the line suit on the top floor of the ship. Why don't we pick our rooms and of course Big Mo, you will have to sleep on the sofa since there are only two bedrooms and you know you and me ain't happening."

"Since we had only a hotdog for lunch I know you are as hungry as I am, but as you know, I cannot go out and about on this ship. I am depending on you guys to keep me nourished, and please take my thermal bottle with you and bring me back hot caffeine coffee with a little sugar and plenty cream. I will relax until you get back with my dinner. We have a time schedule for the formal dining room if that is where you want to eat. I have always preferred the open self serve style eating. If you don't mind, stop by the roast beef area, Big Mo you know how much I like roast beef."

No sooner than they reached the deck, Gunsta Pete spotted Samantha standing at the roast beef stand but dressed for the formal dining room. She looks exactly like her picture, beautiful. Their eyes met as if it was love at first sight. He was with his lady friend and couldn't make a move on her or even introduce himself. Gunsta Pete also thought about waiting for further instructions on how and when to get involved with her. Ms. B will brief him on how to work it. I think that I am going to like her company, after all she is a beautiful woman, and if she wants to break me off a little piece I will be a happy man.

They're back in the suite with Ms. B and plenty to talk about. Gunsta Pete couldn't wait to start talking. "Ms. B, you will never guess who we saw out on the food court." "Samantha Skye." "How did you know, you were not there." "Number one, the excitement in your voice and number two is, there is nothing more important than Samantha's whereabouts at this time. Why are you looking so bent out of shape, Ms. Thang? Don't tell me, I can answer that one too but I ain't going to."

"I see you guys brought back dessert for yourselves. While you all are enjoying your dessert, I will be enjoying my dinner, but first I've got to have a sip of this coffee. Mmmm, just the way I like my coffee, a little sugar and plenty cream, unlike the way I dig my men, strong and black although there is nothing wrong with the "other." Do you think the "other" can handle this strong, black, gorgeous, woman? Nothing's impossible. Listen to me getting carried away with myself. Okay everybody, let's make ourselves comfortable as we eat and talk."

"Ok posse, it looks like everything is running smoothly, so far. It is time for us to make our first move. Remember to never let your guard down. Both you guys will attend the meet and greet social for singles which should start in just a little while.

We two ladies will wait for you here. Gunsta Pete, if you should meet her and hit it tonight, make sure it's just a sample until the next date. Once we know we got her, then you can hit-it and quit-it and go on back to doing your little thing with Ms.Thang here. Get at it you two hunks, be the studs you know you are."

The two ladies go to their separate spaces as expected to wait for Big Mo and Gunsta Pete to come back with a report of their accomplishments for tonight. Like always there were more married men at the social get acquainted event for singles than there were single men. Make you want to go, mmmmm. Both men made their circle around the room but Samantha is nowhere to be seen. The two decided to split up and tour the ship going in different directions. Gunsta Pete entered the jazz club and BAM! There she was, sitting alone sipping on a glass of wine. He went over to where she was sitting and asked her if he may sit next to her and she said to him, "sure." That was the start of something new.

"My name is Gunsta Pete, thank you for sharing your space with me. "You're welcome, my name is Samantha Skye." "Please to meet you, Mrs. Skye." "It's Ms. Skye, and I want you to call me Samantha." "Samantha, it is a pleasure to meet such a beautiful woman. Are you alone on this cruise?" "Yes I am, what about you, are you traveling alone on this cruise, Gunsta Pete?" "I will have to say no on that question, Samantha. I am not married but I am on this cruise with my lady friend. If I had known that I would meet someone like you, I would be alone so that I may enjoy this cruise with you. I know we will be docking tomorrow morning and I will have to take the time to go sight-seeing with my friend. Samantha, will you please allow me to call on you tomorrow night, I enjoy your company and I don't want it to stop." Gunsta Pete, I would love to spend more time with you, and tomorrow night is a date, I'll be waiting for you." "May I escort you back to your suite?" "All I have is a small room with a balcony, but of course with your lady friend and yourself, I'm sure you have a luxury suite." Gunsta Pete just smiled as Samantha led him toward the elevator. Once they got to her door, he acted like a gentleman, kissing her on her hand and said to her, until tomorrow night, will 7pm be okay?" "Yes, that time is good." "See you then, goodnight, lovely lady."

It is midnight and both Big Mo and Gunsta Pete are back in their suite with the ladies. Ms. B. has a million questions to ask and she is looking directly at Gunsta Pete. "Gunsta Pete, from that big wide smile on your face I would guess correctly if I said that you met Samantha Skye tonight and things went well." "Well is what I am waiting to hear about. Did you score with the bitch?" "Just a damn minute, Ms. Thang, we are here on serious business and what Gunsta Pete should have done was to just leave your jealous ass at home."

"The floor is yours, Mr. Gunsta Pete, and please don't excite Ms. Thang over there." "Brown Sugar, as you have already guessed, I did meet Samantha Skye earlier this evening. I must say we hit it off very well although I told her that I was not traveling alone. The fact that I was not traveling alone did not bother her at all. Me having a lady companion seemed to turn her on. I will be seeing her again tomorrow night, we have a date." "Good for you, this may be your only chance to get in deep enough to turn her on and out in a way to make her want to keep you coming back for more. I want you to be in the position to bring her straight to the hands of the authorities so she can start paying for the kidnapping of Lacy and Imani Ball's twin girls. Anyway it is late, I am tired, goodnight, folks."

FIRST ISLAND STOP FOR TOURING

....

All parties of the posse left the ship except Ms. B. They could not take a chance on her being seen by Samantha. So far everything is running smoothly and they don't want to mess that up. Gunsta Pete was very stern with his lady friend about her jealous ways and reminded her of the reason they are on the cruise. He also assured her that she will not be neglected in bed and that Samantha is just another assignment for profit.

"Tiffany, we are touring the Island as a couple so I don't think Samantha will approach me while I am with you. I told her at our first meeting that I was not on this cruise alone." "Gunsta, it's not that I don't believe you or trust you, it's just this crazy jealous feeling I get, knowing that you're with that beautiful woman." "What I see is a dangerous woman. I will never take my attention away from the truth, no matter how charming the beast. Baby, someday you and I will get married, I am counting on it."

While Big Mo, Gunsta Pete and Tiffany were enjoying their sightseeing on the Island, Ms. B was busy roaming the decks of the ship. It's a big risk that she may regret later because she doesn't know who may recognize her on that big ship. She doesn't know if Samantha got off the ship to tour the Island or not. Ms. B had often repeated herself to the posse to be careful and not to take Samantha for granted and that she is a dangerous woman. How could she not follow her own advice about the danger of Samantha Skye. One stupid wrong move and it's trouble, trouble, trouble. Anyway, it's too late to undo what has been done, in other words, you can't turn back the hands of time. Ms. B took advantage of the full day alone to roam the ship and went on a shopping spree, a visit to the spa for a full body massage and a facial which made her feel relaxed. She went back to her suite long enough to get dressed in one of the outfits she bought at the boutique aboard the ship and headed out for a little fun. She spent about an hour in the bar drinking and listening to music. Later, Ms. B went to the roast beef station and got several slices and put together a big juicy Dagwood sandwich before heading back to her suite carrying a large glass of pop to go with her sandwich. By the time the posse returned from their tour of the Island, Ms. B was in bed resting from her long day of adventure.

Ms. B wasn't sure if she should tell the rest of the posse about her day out on deck. She had told everybody she would be staying in the cabin until they returned from their tour of the island. She also knew the danger of being seen by Samantha, which would put them all in great danger. As Ms. B thought about her day she went into deep thought concerning the past few hours on deck of the cruise ship, "What have I done? I knew damn well this day was entirely wrong and yet I put my black ass out there and exposed myself without one m*****f***** thought about the people I could possibly hurt. I sure as hell hope Samantha went on that Island tour like most of the people aboard this ship."

Ms. B braised herself for a tongue lashing as she thought about how and what words to use as she spill out all about her misconduct on behalf of everybody's safety aboard the cruise ship where that Ms. Samantha is concerned. "Right now, I feel like eating my own words, "Never trust a killer and never, ever turn your back on one, and always practice a watchful eye of your enemy", and in my case, Samantha Skye. Right now, at this precise moment, I feel like kicking my own ass. Too bad my foot won't reach back that far."

MS. B'S BIGGEST MISTAKE EVER

....

After everybody returned to the ship from the island tour, there was a lot of feedback about the tour of the Island. They talked about all that they had observed, the unusual things and sites that they had never seen before, and the ways of the Islanders. Nobody had a clue that Ms. B ever left the room while they were out touring the island. Even they know that to leave the cabin would be Ms. B's biggest mistake ever if she is seen on that ship. A bad move like that could get her an ass whipping just for being stupid alone, not counting the good sense she carries around in that fat head of hers. Ms. B decided to speak up and admit to the posse what she had done while they were out touring the Island. "Everybody, there is something I want to tell all of you. Please don't hate me for what I am about to tell you. You will not like it and I want to say to you that I am sorry for what I have done. I have no excuse for what I have done to all of us. I just hope that I have not put our lives in danger, especially you, Gunsta Pete." As Ms. B continued to tell her story nobody said a word. There was only anger on Big Mo's face. The whole room was in silence for a while. Suddenly, there was a roar like the sound of thunder that made everybody stand at attention in silent fear.

Big Mo did not bite his tongue as he spoke with a firm tone in his voice to Ms. B. "Ms. B, I sincerely hope that Samantha was in her room while you were out roaming the decks of this ship. You're the only person she knows in our group, excluding Gunsta Pete. What in hell were you thinking to have done a bull shit trick like that? It never entered my mind that you would turn into an untrustworthy selfish bitch. Woman, at this moment I could kill your no-good back stabbing black ass because that is exactly what you were trying to do to us." "Big Mo, believe me when I say that I am sorry about what I have done, and I hope that I have not jeopardized the lives of my friends. I pray Samantha didn't see me. I promise you, I will not leave this room again until we are docked on American turf, I am steadfast praying that the woman left the ship for tour today." Gunsta Pete's girlfriend spoke up right away, "as a matter of fact, we did see Samantha while we were sightseeing today. Gunsta Pete pointed her out to me. She is a beautiful woman and I felt a little jealous when I saw her. I suppose you can relax now, Ms. B because there is no way Samantha could have seen you, so you are safe from that episode you pulled."

Late evening when all the passengers were back on the ship, the posse began to make plans for the evening. As the ship left the dock headed for the next island, everyone in the suite had a sound of urgency in their voices. Ms. B spoke first, "The only reason for this cruise is to bring Samantha to justice. If we had waited for the authorities to grab her she would have disappeared and went on with her life as if nothing had ever happened. With the law things can be slow because everything has to be in order with the proper paperwork, otherwise she might go free on technicality. For us, siege and capture means nothing but "let's get her devious ass."

Big Mo, Gunsta Pete and Tiffany went out to get dinner and bring it back to the suite so we can continue with the conversation and plans before the next tour stop. "I know what I did was a stupid act on my behalf, but as Ms. Thang said, Samantha was on tour off ship so there was no way she could have seen me while I was touring the ship but we do need to take precaution because we can't take even the little things for granted when it comes to a dirty minded person like Samantha Skye. She has nothing to lose, and she will kill you. As everybody begin to eat the food Big Mo and Gunsta Pete brought back to the cabin, there was a moment of silence for a short time when suddenly Ms. B spoke and broke the silence with something important to say."

"Gunsta Pete, while you are with Samantha and you feel the slightest bit of danger, get away from her as quickly as possible because you will not get a second chance with her. A person who is capable of kidnapping is also capable of murder, and don't you ever drop your guard and forget it."

After dinner, Big Mo and Gunsta Pete got dressed and went out for the evening. The two men soon separated after leaving the suite. Big Mo went to the casino deck and Gunsta Pete headed for Samantha's cabin. He stopped by a bar on the ship nearest to deck where Samantha's cabin is located and bought a bottle of the ship's fine wines to give his lady of the evening, along with an expensive gift he purchased for her while touring the island they had just left. That left Ms. B and Ms. Thang, as Ms. B likes to call her, to spend another night alone in their suite again. They both will go to their own private space and pretend that they each are all alone as they always do.

"Well Ms. Thang, I think we need to spend this time we have together and iron out our differences and our attitudes toward each other. Since we have been living together on this ship in close quarters, I have learned from observing you that you are not a bad person. As a matter of fact, I have learned that you are a person from whom I can benefit by having you in my life.

Ms. Thang, you are a good person and from now on Ms. Thang, you will be treated differently by me. I would like it very much if you would allow me to give you a big hug. As a matter of fact, why don't we give each other a big hug in harmony, my friend"? "Ms. B I have always known that you were not such a bad woman, and I am happy to know that I have won you over. Woman to woman, I think we have found a lifetime friendship, give me another big hug. Girlfriend, I knew you had a big heart when you spoke up to take the worry off me concerning Samantha seeing me aboard this ship. If you are worried or have issues concerning your man you can talk to me, and don't you worry about a thing when it comes to Samantha and Gunsta Pete. The man is just doing his job, and giving her a good lay is a part of the job, and when she is doing him, however and whatever, those are his perks." "In other words, this is a man's world, as the Father of Soul, James Brown sings it." "You know that I have been on both sides of that fence so I am down with it all and there is no shame in my game."

Twenty

A ROMANTIC EVENING FOR SAMANTHA AND GUNSTA PETE

....

"Good evening G P, don't you look magazine front cover magnificent this evening." "Thank you, madam; as Gunsta Pete smiled with a devilish wink with a sudden, ooooh weee! Baby, as always, I am standing here looking at an angel, and that outfit you're wearing girl, you are a drop-dead-brick-house-knockout." Both laughed as they left for the main dining room.

After stuffing themselves on two helpings of lobster and lobster rice dish, they took a stroll to a cozy bar aboard the ship. After downing a bottle of wine, they decided to go dancing and went to a night club where the band was playing oldies music. "Samantha, the music is great, it takes me back to my high school days. I don't know about you but the rhythm is going through my bloodstream and I feel good inside out." It must have been something in his attitude because Samantha became very much alarmed, and she spoke up; G P, I can see the ladies looking at you with those needy eyes and I don't plan to share you with none of them. You will not meet any of those whores' funky needs tonight. Beast of mankind, you are all mine tonight, all night."

By midnight, Samantha and Gunsta Pete were back at Samantha's cabin. They both were good and high and very horny. "Samantha, my dear lady, are you feeling what I am feeling at this moment?" "G P, my body is feeling the need to release some juices that only comes with orgasms, and that is what I am feeling a need for right now." "That is an invitation I can't resist, and baby, know that your needs will be met."

BAD, BAD WHISKY MADE ME LOSE MY HAPPY LIFE

....

After sometime knocking boots and satisfying the flesh of the horny beast, Samantha and Gunsta Pete took a break and relaxed, sipping on vodka and their favorite juices. As the two drank the night away and talking, things begin to change with Gunsta Pete. The drinks seem to take control of the tongue. "Samantha, I think that I am having strong attachment feelings toward you. I think I am falling in love with you." "G P, I know that I am falling in love with you."

The more they sipped on their drinks, the more Gunsta Pete rambled on and on and on about nothing important that would get Samantha's attention. As with honesty and drunks, the truth will eventually come out and bite you. And, as sure as shit stinks the time came quickly. "What, what!" Samantha has just listened to Gunsta Pete mumble something about a plan to have her brought back to the U.S.A. for kidnapping. As Samantha looks over at Gunsta Pete, her mind is in deep thought, "I am going to kill your conniving black ass, Mr. Gunsta Pete, and lying there, you're just as good as dead." Good happy drinking took a nose dive.

EARLY MORNING ABOARD SHIP

6 O'CLOCK A.M.

....

"Good morning, Big Mo and Ms.Thang, where is Gunsta Pete this morning?" Big Mo spoke up with a chuckle, "It looks like Gunsta Pete is sleeping in late this morning." "Ms. Thang, did you overwork him when he got back from his date with Samantha last night?" "Ms. B, he did not come home from his date last night, and I am pissed. It is one thing to share him with another woman for a good cause, but to stay on it all night long means he is sho-nuff enjoying it. His lie to me was that nobody could lay it on him the way I can. I guess he has found another great sex partner, and as far as I am concerned he can stay on it until the cows come home, he's all hers now. Ms. B and Big Mo, I am not blaming either one of you because it was a contracted deal and he is smart enough to know how far to go with the enemy even if he is enjoying it." "Ms. Thang, I do understand how you must feel not having your man here with you, but I know there has to be a good reason behind this." "Ms. B is right, Tiffany, there has to be a good reason for this because I know my dog, and he would be in touch with me unless something was wrong." "Ms. B, do you have something in mind to ease our minds?" "What I have in mind is for the two of you to go out and cover this ship from top to bottom and don't stop searching until you have found Gunsta Pete. We must find him before our next stop of this cruise. If either of you should see Samantha, please bring her to me, and she will tell us where our partner is, I guarantee it."

"It is almost midday and there is no sign of Gunsta Pete. Ms. Thang, I know this is hard for you and Big Mo, I know Gunsta Pete is your man. I did not count on a disappearance and now I must organize a search party and get to the bottom of Samantha's little game before we get to the next island of our tour on the cruise."

After a long day combing the ship searching for Gunsta Pete, Ms. B, Ms. Thang and Big Mo have all become unnerved. There has been no sign of Samantha and the ship's authorities have no reason to search her room. The reason for this is because there has not been a report on Gunsta Pete being missing or his association with Samantha Skye.

"There has been a crime committed on this ship and we can't prove a damn thing. Before we dock tomorrow morning we are going to report what has happened, which will be that our friend, Gunsta Pete is missing. We must be prepared to tell the whole story from the beginning to the present." "Ms. B you already know that Big Mo and I are with you in whatever you decide to do. We got your back at all times, so always know and not guess whether or not you can count on us." "Thanks, both of you, now let's be prepared by making a few phone calls back to the United States."

After a long night, Ms. B, Ms. Thang and Big Mo decided to have a big breakfast before the ship docked on the next scheduled island of their next cruise tour. "Ms. Thang and Big Mo, I must tell you that at this time I am in a place of hysterical worry, and I am scared to death with the thought of what might have happened to Gunsta Pete. I think the three of us should stick together while we are on the island, and maybe for the rest of the trip. As soon as we are back on the ship, the three of us are going to see the captain so that he can put the ship's security people on the case. Something tells me that Samantha will be leaving the ship and my plan is that we follow her and find out if she is with someone else and who is this person on the ship with her."

THE SEARCH GOES ON

....

After involving the ship's captain and the ship's security team, Ms. B feels that the right decision has been made. "I feel like we are missing something but I can't put a handle on it. Did any of you see Samantha while you were touring the Island?" "As a matter of fact, I did see Samantha and I pointed her out to Tiffany. She was touring the Island alone. I should have forced her to tell me the whereabouts of Gunsta Pete.

As always, after the tour of the island, there is a big meeting and instructions for the next move on Samantha. This time it is about their concern about the whereabouts of Gunsta Pete. There is no doubt in everybody's mind that Samantha has done harm to him and the remaining posse members will get to the bottom of it. “I am just as angry as I am scared. If they don’t find Gunsta Pete, Samantha Skye is just as good as dead or my name ain’t Brown Sugar. If Samantha is hiding, she had better be the only one who knows the secret place otherwise her ass is history”. Big Mo spoke up, “It’s amazing how she made herself very visible on each island tour but unseen on the ship. We should have been following her and keeping a closer eye on the subject. We should have studied her the way she studied the people she considered her enemies, and made note of all actions of movements with that woman every step of the way. It looks like Samantha was at least one step ahead of us all along. The question now is, how do we even begin to try to think like her satanic mind? We may be bad, but neither of us is all bad.”

THE BREAK IN

…………………..

After all night, meeting, planning and plotting Ms. B came up with the idea that maybe they should watch Samantha’s cabin and when she comes out to go for breakfast they will enter her room and look for evidence on the whereabouts of Gunsta Pete. “Big Mo, I want you and Ms. Thang to stay together because there has to be someone’s eyes on Samantha at all times and one of you will have to call me on my cell phone from your cell phone when she is headed back to her room. I will be looking around in her room for clues on our missing friend. My toughest job will be to convince the person who cleans her room that I spent the night there and when I left for breakfast, I forgot something and I can't find Samantha who is with her male friend this morning.

After waiting nearby for almost an hour, there is no sign of Samantha and everybody is getting tired of waiting. Ms. B came up with a clever idea. "Ms. Thang, I want you to go knock on her door and when she answers, tell her you are looking for your friend, Gunsta Pete and you're asking everybody he has talked with, and that he had mentioned that he had met her when you guys were out touring." Her knocks went unanswered and another plan quickly went into place. Ms. B sent Tiffany to talk with the ship authorities about what they suspect while she convinced Big Mo that they should go in and do a search on their own.

"Remember Big Mo, we've got to get in and out of Samantha's cabin as quickly as possible, and if she is in here, so be it." "Ms. B, it was a good idea to have Tiffany visit the security office to chat with the guys for a little while, we know she's safe there." "Big Mo, something is wrong here, just look around here and tell me what you see." "Ms. B. if the closet is as empty as this room, I can clearly say that this cabin is unoccupied and if this is true, where in the hell is Samantha"? What Big Mo and Ms. B does know, is that Samantha did get off the ship, but what they do not know is that she did not get back on the ship. Also, what Big Mo and Tiffany failed to observe was the two wheeler carry-on that she had with her and putting the little things she was buying such as Islanders wear (sundresses) and soaps, sweet smells and hair products, all just a trick to make them think that she was having a good time shopping. What they didn't know was that Samantha was observing them. It's like the old wise saying, "you can't out-fox a fox." She already had needed items, including make-up in her two wheeler carry-on. Her escape was well planned and nothing and no one on this side of hell was going to interfere or stop her well thought out plans.

"Big Mo, it looks like we have a real mystery on our hands with the sign of murder. I know that we don't know how to solve it or go about putting this mystery puzzle together to even try to begin to put it together. Do you have any thoughts in mind, my man?" "I'm afraid to speak what is on my mind because it will come out suspected murderer naming you-know-who every time." "You know Big Mo, we cannot reveal what we suspect or think we know because we should not be in this room. All we can do is wait for the authorities on this ship to reveal what they came up with. Either way, I don't think we will leave this ship with Gunsta Pete walking off with us. Somehow Samantha has managed to make his body disappear, and she is gone also. Where could she possibly be hiding? I don't know where the answers lie, but I do know they must be and will be answered. You can think of it as written in blood."

It is early morning, and with the ship nearing home destination, and there is still no answers about their complaint on their missing friend, and all parties are wondering why. "All three of us need to visit the security office before we dock. We want answers before we leave this ship. Hell, we demand an answer on this matter before we leave this ship." "I'm with you all the way, Ms. B. The time I spent with the security guys while you and Big Mo were doing the search in Samantha's cabin was very interesting. They said that they had searched every inch of the ship except any of the sleeping quarters. They may be doing that just as we speak. They plan to knock on cabin room doors, but first they will ask Samantha to leave the room while they do a complete search since she is being accused of a wrong and also suspected of wrong doing." "I am very happy to hear that they are on it and I thank you for your part in helping us, Ms. Thang. Let's eat breakfast and double check our sleeping quarters before we dock."

Before they could leave their suite there was a knock on the door. Big Mo opened the door and two young men from the security team stepped in and pleasantly asked them all to have a seat, and that they needed to talk to them. Ms. B blurted out, "Lord, have mercy; I know you have come to bring us bad news." After the two men sat down, one of them spoke up and said to them that they would prefer to wait for someone else who will be joining them. Suddenly, there was another knock at the door, and this time one of the security men answered it. "I want you all to meet Dr. Day, who is part of the ship's staff. Dr. Day will be sitting in with us while I talk to you. Ms. B blurted out,

"Now I know there is something wrong, please tell us now, don't do this to us. Tell us now or get the hell out now, I mean it, get out of here now. You have failed us and you don't know how to tell us, so just get up and go."

As one of the men began to talk, the room became quiet. "We searched Samantha Skye's cabin early this morning and there was no sign of Ms. Skye but we did find another person in her cabin. We need one of you to identify him." Ms. B blurted out in an intense sounding voice, "what do you mean identify him, what in hell are you trying to tell us, just say it. Tell us now, is he badly hurt, is he dead or what?" Dr. Day observed carefully each of them as they braised themselves for the worse.

"We noticed right away that there was no sign of anyone staying in that cabin. We turned the place up side down and just as we were about to leave, I opened the patio door that leads to the balcony, and to my surprise there was this man lying there on a lounge chair with the appearance of sleeping. It didn't take us long before it was obvious that he was not sleeping, as a matter of fact, the smell of death had already set in from being exposed to the sun out on the balcony." Ms. B quickly spoke up, "And you said that there was no sign of Samantha, and also there was no sign of her ever being in that cabin, is that what I am hearing? Usually, a woman will leave some kind of sign, something from her makeup case or something." "I am so sorry, but there were no signs of anyone in that cabin, except a dead man's body. Please, we need one of you to come with us to identify the body." Big Mo spoke up right away, "I'll go with you to identify the body." "Thank you sir, we will go to the ship's makeshift morgue where we are holding the body."

BACK ON THE ISLAND

Samantha has already established herself on the island by using an old friend's identification; Samantha's friend who once lived on the island, but moved back to the states, got married and changed her name so Samantha can hide behind her friend's maiden name. Samantha found a house to her liking and rented it right away. Because the living is not very high, her money will go a long way on the island, at least until she ropes in an islander sucker, and as we already know, there are fools everywhere all day long, especially the ones they call pussy fools and vagina-a-holics.

"Good evening, neighbors. My name is, Karley Jone. I moved from the other side of the island and I must say this is a beautiful neighborhood. I promise you, this house will be well kept, and my visitors will be those who are respectable." Samantha's instant thought was, "I now have won and am now a free woman and have beat those bitches at their own lousy games. They all will know that nobody messes over me and go on living like nothing ever happened."

The demon pranced into her new found home feeling on top of the world. As she walked through admiring the beauty of the décor she entered the bedroom and slowly taking in all the beauty when suddenly her eyes fell upon the bed. Feeling a little apprehended she slowly walked over to the bed to get a closer look and proceeded to pick up the sheet of paper with writing on it. As Samantha began to read what was written, it was obvious fear had consumed her face but she continued to read, "Hello! Let me introducc myself, I am The Reaper, the mirror to your soul's keeper, I am here to collect what you have sowed and to let you know what is further down the road. If what you have sowed is on the dark side, you have chosen satanic demons to be your guide. Your negative actions are birthed through negative thoughts, and a sinner as yourself will reap of all your corrupted faults, so see it like it is as you watch your life unfold, and know that it is too late for your sinful ass to unload. You weaved your life into a detrimental state and now your lousy soul is consumed with hate. But don't give up, Samantha, your life is not yet lost, try praying for forgiveness and the strength to pay the cost. Samantha stood there at her bedside like a zombie, frozen stiff.

Twenty One

SCARED AS HELL AND NO PLACE TO RUN

....

The fear in Samantha has her talking to herself, and it is a good thing all the windows are shut tight, otherwise the neighbors would think she is really off her rocker. She begin to, ask herself questions and yet there are no answers for her. "Who is this person or persons who are aware of me and I am not aware of them? I am not aware of anyone and I have not been told about a possible acquaintance here on the Island when my friend gave me this place to stay. Here on the Island, I have no place to run and hide like when I was in the States."

Samantha immediately went to a hardware store and she bought new locks for the house, including a lock for her bedroom door. She noticed that during the daylight hours everybody is out and around. The children are busy into their activities of games and play and the adults are busy with their daily routines, which put a great idea in her mind. As her thoughts became verbal, "Daytime may be the best time for me to sleep because, with all the hustle and bustle of the day there might be less criminal activities with, all these people lurking around. I will sleep during the daytime and be watchful during the night."

Samantha continued mumbling to herself, "I am so happy that I am handy with some things. A single woman, almost have to be, a jack-of-all-trades, type person. I will do all my work around this house, including installing new locks, outside and inside. I will live in seclusion until I figure out what my next step will be. Nobody will be allowed in my house. I don't know who my enemy on this Island is, but I do know I got to find a way to get away as soon as possible. It is living hell when the game doesn't know the hunter."

"Whoever the person is or persons are, has to know who I am with connection to someone who wants me out the way for some reason. Who knows, it could be someone who lost her husband during the time I was in his life. Some men are just too stupid and don't have sense enough to know that home front has to be kept well and, in tact and, with satisfaction that is laid solid. A man has to know that when he gets up off that thing and he hasn't met her satisfaction, someone can and will lend a hand and give a little help. One of those men may have stayed off that thing a little too long while fooling around with me and, it's like, "mama don't play that", and now her ass is after me. Maybe, it's her, or even a hired hit-man, or whatever the case might be, my fine ass has been scheduled for eternal rest and I am not ready to go. I got a lot of living to do. All my energy starting tonight will be spent on a plan to leave the Island as soon as possible. My chance to hook an Islander sucker is no longer possible since I can't trust, nobody, here on this Island."

ONE PHOTO AND THE WHOLE STORY IS TOLD IN LIVING COLOR

....

"If it was a snake it would have bitten me," were the words that burst out of Samantha's mouth as she bent down and picked up a picture that was sticking out from beneath a piece of furniture in her bedroom. As she looked at the picture she could not believe what she was seeing as the shock appeared on her face resembling that of pure fear.

"Yeeeeeeeeeeee," was all that came out of Samantha's mouth as she clutched the picture she had picked up from the floor. On the picture in living color is that of her friend Karley Jone, the person whose identity she has taken over while staying on the Island. It is a wedding picture of Karley and her first husband. The man in the picture with her is the same man Samantha was with when she was living in a suburban area in New York. Samantha mumbled, "I was with him before and after his divorce. I had no idea he was Karley's husband. She has set me up and I fell right into her trap. All I can say at this time is, Lord, please, have mercy on me, I need it."

Samantha decided to not take anything with her that would cause her to need a suitcase. Until she gets off the Island, she will carry her regular large size purse that she has been carrying since her arrival on the Island. She will take only clothing that will fit in her purse without causing alarm to someone who may be following and watching her. So that she does not have to open her bag when she needs ID or money, she will keep those things in her pocket, which is beautifully styled in the upscale fashion design she will be wearing when she has to leave the house. In her head, she can hear her own thoughts verbalized in words coming from her mouth. She begins to pray with tears streaming down her face.

MEMORIAL SERVICE FOR GUNSTA PETE

....

Back in Detroit, at Brown Sugar's Beauty Salon, Ms. B started calling all her friends and Big Mo started calling his other posse members. It was not something Ms. B could talk about on the phone, so she had everybody come to her place of business. She also called Sergeant Troyer because she knew that the Sergeant was in charge of the Ball's case when their twin daughters were kidnapped.

"I am so glad you all could come to my place of business today, thank you so much for coming. As you know, I just came back from a cruise with the posse. We were following Samantha Skye to see what she was up to and to make the report to you through a Detective name Virg Lanne, of my findings, Sergeant Troyer. I want everybody to be patient with me because I have a story to tell you."

After Ms. B finished talking, Lacy Ball stood up and made an announcement and his wife, Imani stood beside him. Lacy announced that he wanted everybody in the room to come to the Ball's mansion on Saturday, a week from tomorrow to attend a memorial service for Gunsta Pete. He told them that only the people from Ms. B's shop and Gunsta Pete's family members will be invited to come to the service. Lacy said that he wanted to do something honorable for the man who put his life on the line to bring the terrible woman to justice.

"My best friend, who is with me today, has proven that he is100% true friend. He financially sponsored the cruise including the flight to Florida and money needed to get the job done. He is the one who hired the private detective, Virg Lanne to find my twin daughters when Samantha kidnapped them. Will you please come up and stand with me, also your beautiful wife, who is also my wife's best friend. Ladies and gentlemen, two of the Metro's best, Attorney Tyrone Haywill and his wife, Mrs. Monique Haywill. They are a blessing in our lives."

A WEEK LATER, SATURDAY MORNING
At the Ball's Mansion

....

"Good morning, I am very happy to see all of you here this morning and on time, if I may say. We will go ahead and get started." Lacy turned to Ms. B. and speaking with a soft voice, he said to her, "Ms. B, I will turn the program over to you, and please let the guest know that breakfast will be served immediately after service." Ms. B looked into Lacy's face and spoke softly, "Thank you Mr. Ball, and thank Imani for me, and most of all, thank you for allowing me in your home and not bringing up the past about Imani and me."

"Good morning, everybody, I am known as Ms. B, the owner of Brown Sugar's Beauty Salon. It was at my place of business where I first met Mr. Gunsta Pete. He came into my salon one day with his buddy, who is also my friend, known as Big Mo, and from that day on he was always dropping by just to say hello to my girls and Luscious and to give a holler at me. I always knew that I could count on him if I ever needed him, and that is why he was on the cruise ship with me and Big Mo. The two are a part of a group called the posse and they always had my back and I could always call on them when I needed them. They looked out for hard working business people like me. I knew Samantha was a dangerous woman and we used all precautions to safeguard ourselves from her tricks. Gunsta Pete was doing something good by helping a friend and he lost his life in the process of bringing the lowlife to justice. Since the incident, I have been hurting and I know you are too, and I am asking that we all keep a prayer on our hearts for each other. There is someone who is not here this morning, I call her Ms. Thang but her name is Tiffany. She was Gunsta Pete's companion on the cruise. She is not here because she is going through a rough time over Gunsta Pete's death. He was the love of her life and now she has lost him in death from murder. Please add her to your prayer list. I am also asking the family members of Gunsta Pete to please give me a picture of him to hang in my salon as a reminder of our friend and hero. I will now give our guest and friends of the decease the honor of coming up to speak, and afterward, breakfast will be served."

A WRAP-UP AT THE PRECINCT
8:00 A.M.

……………………………………………

"Thank you, Mr. and Mrs. Ball for coming in this morning for this conference. As you have learned, Samantha has disappeared, perhaps on one of the islands abroad when the ship docked. You also heard about the man who was found murdered in her room. Although you didn't know him, you heard about him and the part he played in your lives. We also know that Samantha presented herself as a dangerous woman from past encounters with her and that she is capable of committing murder. And that is what happened to the man we knew as Gunsta Pete, who was found murdered in Samantha's cabin aboard the cruise ship. He was there to deliver her to the hands of authorities once he and his companions reached American soil. There had to be concrete evidence on hand for the authorities to take her into custody and Samantha was not wasting any time getting away from her evil-minded actions and the evil-doer proved to be one step ahead, but she can and will be caught."

"We thank you from the bottom of our hearts for all that you have done to help us, Detective Troyer, and we truly mean it. Knowing this makes both Imani and me feel good about so many people caring about us. I would like to stay in touch with you from time to time." "I would be happy to hear from the two of you from time to time. Why don't we drop the former address for each other and call me Mary." "Mary, our new found friend, we want, you to call us Imani and Lacy. This is going to be a beautiful friendship, isn't it, my dear wife?"

Back to the norm

....

The Haywill family is back to their normal weekly routines. Angel and Ty, Jr. both have notice a difference in the atmosphere around the house. Monique and Tyrone are more playful with each other instead of looking and talking seriously about things children can't be in the presence of or be involved in. The weekend will be a joyous time for everybody when they all get together at the Ball Mansion for friends get-together. Angel and Ty, Jr. like socializing with the Ball twins, Lacey and Stacey and they are happy about all the good changes happening in their lives. They have been given more freedom to do and to also go places that they were formerly doing as a norm in their everyday lives.

The family dinner seem to be taking on more time than Monique and Tyrone wanted as they all engaged in conversations while eating one of Angel and Ty, Jr.'s favorite dishes which is Monique's famous homemade, Spaghetti sauce with Ground Turkey, made from her own special ingredients, poured over spaghetti, and served with cheese bread, which is also homemade. "Kids, I have really enjoyed this great conversation, especially after realizing you both quietly continued your lives without causing a disruption with me and your dad. Of course, if we had known you were making grownup decisions for yourselves, we would never have allowed it." Tyrone interrupted Monique, "Monique, it sounds to me like our son and daughter have grown up right before our eyes and we, their parents, were too busy to see the change." "Tyrone, does that mean that we need to give them more rope length of freedom to spread their wings a little more and to be trusted with more decisions in their lives?" "Yes, Monique, and we can discuss this later and call a family meeting so that they will understand our expectations of them with our trust and understanding concerning them." After dinner, everyone cheerfully said their goodnight to each other and went to their private quarters for the rest of the evening, since it was already late because of a late dinner and long dinner talk.

Just a short time later, things have already started happening in the master bedroom of Tyrone and Monique. After getting ready for bed and before cutting off the lights, Tyrone beckoned for Monique's attention. He has written a song and he wants to try it out with Monique. He puts his arms around her and gives her a smooth kiss on her lips. He then takes her over to his favorite chair and sits her down. Before she could ask him questions, he started singing to her,

"The first time I saw you my love
I wanted you to be mine, my love
The essence of your presence surrenders me
Right where I need to be and my body yearns to be

Oh baby, this is real, your TKO I can feel
That is why I know that this time it is real
You're all that I dream of and all that I need
Just let me hold you and kiss you and lo----ve you baby Because this time, oh baby, this time for me, oh, oh, oh, oh, o----h Oh baby I know that this time it is real."

Monique was without words for a moment, and she was showing the love bug all over her face. "Sweetheart, have I told you lately that I love you?" "Yes dear, and I like hearing you say it to me. I am also waiting for you to show me how much you love me." "Don't worry yourself about it my dear sweet baby, because it's coming, you have no idea how it's coming. Why don't you make yourself comfortable while I pour up a couple glasses of our favorite wine mixed with a splash of our, "get freaky" sidekick, better still, why don't we continue in the bedroom, and Monique, don't you even think about putting on a gown, I want you to go to the bedroom and prepare yourself for a little piece of heaven." As soon as Monique left the room, Tyrone made a call on his cell phone. After talking for a few minutes he stood up with a broad smile on his face as he walked toward the bedroom. When he entered the bedroom, he walked over to the radio and turned it on. As the song "You're Perfect To Me" by, Al Green, played on the radio, Tyrone walked slowly over to the bed and looked down at Monique, moving his tongue as if he could sap her up like syrup with biscuits on a plate. It was call of the wild, Reddi Whip and all. As Monique beckoned for Tyrone to come down to her, Tyrone spoke in a soft romantic voice saying, "Monique, you are a man's dream come true and I love you." A couple sips from their wine glasses and it (!!!) on and on and on.

Almost an hour later as Monique lay on her back looking at the ceiling, still breathing hard after one of her and Tyrone's husband and wife oneness together, and at the same time she was in deep thought as she reached over and began to soft-touch massage Tyrone along the lower part of his thigh, gentle and slowly working her way to the upper area and with a soft voice she recites a love message to him, "Tyrone baby, lying here close to you in the still of the night, I'm wrapped in the essence of our recent utmost love pleasure height, and sugar, I know that I have your love, that's why I'm counting my blessings, yes, all my blessings from above. The sound of your voice sends love waves up and down my spine, and when you reach out and pull me closer to you, I know my life is in perfect divine, so sugar, my sweet darling, God knows how much I love you. I want to always be your total what, why, when and who, and sugar my sweets, to show you how much I'm in love with you, the whole world can wait in line if there's something you want me to do. If the world should question my being in love, I don't give a damn because sugar, I am." By the time Monique finished talking and maneuvering her soft touches in that sensuous area, it was oops, "baby, I couldn't hold it any longer." "Monique let it slip, "two for you and just one for me." All Tyrone could do was smile. He didn't have the energy at the moment to do nothing more.

Rrrring rrrrring rrrring…..right on time just like Tyrone had planned for the evening, and poor Monique didn't have a clue to what was happening. Tyrone lets Monique answer the phone. "Tyrone, it's a client of yours and he sounds desperate." Tyrone answered the phone quickly, "Hello, this is Attorney Haywill speaking, how may I help you? Oh, I'm sorry to hear that, do you need me to be there with you? Oh no, it is no trouble at all, I'm on my way, just relax yourself and try to stay calm." Tyrone hurriedly showered and dressed and was out of the house on his way to comfort a client. What the hell was on Monique's mind to pass that off as the norm for a lawyer, and, whatever happened to the business side that says "I will see you in my office tomorrow morning," not that bull shit about I'm on my way. By the time the light-bulb switched on in her head she was on her feet but it was too late, Tyrone was already gone. "Where the hell was he going and who was this client on the phone? Was it a setup for him to meet some woman? No, he wouldn't gamble our marriage on that. Anyway I don't think he has the energy after all we just finished doing, and I know the man loves me, every inch of me, the whole size 16 delicious me." Monique drifted off into a deep sleep with a smile on her face.

BETWEEN TWO LOVES

One up & One Down

....

3:00 A.M. at Tyrone Haywill's Law Office

....

Tyrone arrives at his office, and as he walks in and looks around he sees two champagne glasses on his desk surrounded with pretty decorations, and the song, believe it or not, "You're Perfect To Me" by Al Green was playing, engulfing the whole room with those beautiful lyrics. Tyrone heard the whisper of a soft voice behind him, and as he turned he looked his lover in the face. At that magical moment, all Tyrone could say to **him** was "you're perfect to me and I'm so in love with you."

The End

For now, but we'll be back.

!!!

WHEN LOVE HURTS, IT HURTS

!!

HURTING LOVE

HURTING LOVE

When love hurts you know, it's just ain't no good

Yet you keep on hoping and doing all you possibly could

Knowing that your stuff is roaming for another's connection

Acting like a dog in heat with no damn affection or direction

Lust is a hell of a thing when you can't control your shit

And yet still there's that strong desire to hump a little bit

But as we already know, it doesn't last forever

Good sense kicks in and he knows home nest is better

Now he's dragging home with his tail between his "ass"

Stead-fast praying for a chance to forever make it last

And if home is no longer there for him to claim

Maybe **HURTING** love just ain't worth the **PAIN.**

HAYWOOD PUBLISHING, LLC

Visit our website at

www.haywoodbooks.com

Also, let us hear from you at

haywoodpublishing@sbcglobal.net

MAY THE DARKNESS OF DESPAIR TODAY MANIFEST IN YOU, RAYS OF JOY COME DAWN.

LOVE FROM MY HEART TO YOURS,

Floria

TO BE OR NOT TO BE
WHAT, IS THE QUESTION
AM I RIGHT OR AM I WRONG
WHO, IS MY JUDGE
IS IT FOR ME OR IS IT NOT
WHO, IS MY KEEPER
WILL I NEED OR SHOULD I READ
WHO, IS MY TEACHER
SHOULD I STAY OR SHOULD I GO
WHO, WILL SHOW COMPASSION
WILL THERE BE RAIN TOMORROW
WHO, WILL OFFER ME SHELTER
IS, MY HEART OPEN TO UNDERSTANDING
TO WHOM FAITH BRINGS LOVE, PEACE AND
TRANQUILITY.

LIFE IS BEAUTIFUL
KEEP YOUR GIFT FROM GOD

Keep, a look out for Floria's next book, coming soon.

www.ingramcontent.com/pod-product-compliance
Lightning Source LLC
LaVergne TN
LVHW091036080826
845145LV00002B/524